The Abbey Quill Mysteries

The Hopper Rescue

The Agatha Solutions

Alibi for Murder

Elizabeth Eng

BookLocker
Trenton, Georgia

Print ISBN: 978-1-958891-19-3
Ebook ISBN: 979-8-88531-605-7

Published by BookLocker.com, Inc., Trenton, Georgia.

This is a work of fiction. Names, characters, places and incidents are either the products of the author's imagination or are used fictitiously. Any resemblance to actual persons, living or dead, events or locales is entirely coincidental.

BookLocker.com, Inc.
2024

First Edition

Author photo and interior photos were taken by the author.

Author Acknowledgements

Thanks are due for the invaluable assistance of many people who helped make this book a reality. To members of the Wordcrafters, whose constant support in so many ways only made my stories stronger, I look forward to continuing our writing journey together; to Gwen Nelson, who provided valuable feedback on finished manuscripts, my sincere appreciation; and to Keith Eng, who considered the questions I tossed at him and came up with the best solutions, deepest thanks to you.

Also by Elizabeth Eng

For Middle Grade Readers (Ages 8-12):

The Secret of the Tower

For Young Children (Ages 3-6):

Flynn at Home (Illustrated by William Paul Marlette)

For Older Children:

Flynn: Adventures of a Rough Collie (Contains full color photographs of Flynn and a Spanish translation)

The Hopper Rescue

Chapter 1

I had a feeling today would be different. My days at work begin quietly enough. I am always the first to arrive, usually the only person in the building all day. And I love that part of the job. Most people who call me, email me, or ring the bell on the old brick building are pleasant. I do what I can to help them with whatever they need, whether it's something as simple as an address or phone number, or more involved like the date of a baptism. I am Abbey Quill, secretary of the Highland Baptist Church.

My house is on the shore of Lake Ontario, so Monday, Wednesday, and Friday I take the Lake Avenue bus straight south to Genesee Street. I hop off at the corner, stopping at the neighborhood bakery to grab something for breakfast. In the ancient brick, two story building, the Brooks Bakery has been around for decades and is a local favorite. Today, I opened the door, causing the bell hanging from a leather strap to do its thing with a jingle and alert the employee behind the food case to look up.

"Good morning, Abbey! How are you?" Jane's round, freckled face looked delighted to see me. As usual, I had to stop in my tracks and inhale deeply. It was a bakery, after all.

"Great, thanks, and you?" I replied after I had come out of my yeast- and sugar-induced coma.

Jane responded with her usual reply, "I'm here, that's what counts." She finished placing muffins in the case and said, "What can I get for you this morning?"

I was a regular customer, but I didn't have a regular order. Far from it. I never knew what would strike my fancy day to day. Stepping up to the case, I eyed the muffins Jane had just finished arranging. This morning could be a muffin day, but… those croissants looked delicious. "I'll have an almond croissant, please. And how about one of those half-moon cookies?" I set a five-dollar bill on the counter.

"Coming up!" Jane whipped open a white bakery bag and grabbed a tissue with which to pick up my selections. Reaching into the case, she chose a big, flaky croissant and then one of the large, half chocolate, half vanilla frosted round cookies. As I was being waited on, I looked around the shop, making note of the other familiar customers at a couple tables. My eyes rested on the bulletin board. I decided to check it out before leaving.

"Thanks, Jane," I said, as she handed me the bag of pastries. "Make it a great day."

"You, too," she replied, and turned to the person waiting behind her, her face smiling, greeting the next customer.

I made my way over to the wall to read the notices. This was a community board with posts of all kinds, such as announcing upcoming concerts (rock and folk bands and pipe organ) and peaceful demonstrations, yard sales, and Girl Scout cookies being sold in the community center parking lot. The one that caught my attention this morning was an appeal for volunteers at the local animal shelter. The notice was in color and showed a smiling man holding two adorable golden retriever puppies. Okay, so the man was adorable looking, too. It was the one being tacked to the board by a tall man in a navy sport whom I didn't recall seeing before in the store. Wow. The fellow in the picture had bright blue eyes the color of...

"Do you like dogs, cats, bunnies? We could really use some help downtown with the animals," the man next to me said.

"Oh, I don't know if—" I looked up into the two bluest eyes I'd ever seen. Wait. I looked back at the poster. Yup. Same guy. I licked my lips before answering (yes, I really did that). "You know, I'll bet I could smuggle with a puppy or two. I, mean snuggle!" *Geez, was I blithering?* I gazed up at him.

He finished placing the last thumbtack on the flyer and reached out his hand to introduce himself. "Sean. I'm Director of Community Events at the downtown shelter."

I felt a slight charge when our hands met. "Abbey. So nice to meet you," I said. Reluctantly, I let go of the firm handshake. "Uh, I will check my calendar and see when I have free time." I automatically ran a hand through my long dark hair to smooth any stray strands.

"Perfect. Whatever time you can fit in will help." He sighed. "So much to do, and not enough people to do it. Walking the dogs, supplying tech support, you name it, we need it." He stepped toward the door. "Thanks, and hope to see you soon." With a wave he was out of the bakery.

I hope to see you soon, too. Standing there, I allowed my eyes to follow him until he was out of sight. I left the bakery with pastries and a feeling that my life was about to be enhanced in several ways.

As I walked the block to the church, I reflected on meeting Sean. Sure, he was good looking and polite, but did I really want to volunteer at the animal shelter? Even I knew volunteering meant more than cuddling the puppies and kittens. I'd be expected to clean kennels and cages in addition to other duties. On the other hand, I'd really been stuck in a rut since Colin, my last boyfriend, left me. Well, I kicked him out. He thought he could sit at home and do nothing all day. And nothing was just that, nothing, No cooking, no cleaning, no laundry, no yardwork, no maintenance. He was good at keeping the recliner warm, though, and enjoying my cable television and my "housekeeping" tasks. We're both in our late twenties and after being able to purchase my home a few years ago, I became very possessive of it. Colin would call it selfish. Anyway, after a few months, I decided I was not about to be taken advantage of by a slacker of a boyfriend, so goodbye, Colin. No idea where he is now; don't know, don't care.

After climbing the building's cement steps, I took my keys out of my pocket. I loved the fact that they still used the old door locks from decades ago, but it's sad they had to install a security system. The church was broken into a few years back, and the powers that be decided better late than never. The crime in Roc City is ever on the increase. Fortunately, they didn't suffer too much damage to the inside of the church, but the emotional scars are still there. After 100 years they thought they were safe. Shows what can happen when one is complacent. Once I had locked the door behind me, I quickly punched in the four-digit code. The sharp 'beep" reassured me all was secure.

Chapter 2

I picked up last week's mail. Since the mail is delivered after I leave for the day, there's usually a small pile on the floor from where it was pushed through the mail slot, plus whatever is delivered on my days off. I walked through the coat room and unlocked the office door, placed the mail on the desk in a short stack, and stashed my purse in the desk. Then I started up the coffee maker and the computer. Finally, I made my way back to the hallway.

My workday always included a short stop in the sanctuary. I occupied my usual seat in the second row, before the steps leading to the altar. War, greed, poverty, inequality. These injustices all needed a moment of meditation before I started dealing with church business. After a brief reflection, I walked slowly back up the aisle from the pew, taking in the impressive walls of colorful windows and lovingly polished wainscoting. With its huge stained-glass windows, wooden pews and soft maroon carpeting, the sanctuary surely is a place of respite. Built in 1921, the building's architecture is a brick collegiate cathedral style. Think old Ivy League college campuses. They don't make them like this anymore.

It would be so easy for me to tarry in the comfort of this splendid room, but I needed to get busy. No doubt the phone would start ringing and emails begin pinging soon, so I went back to the office and took my place at the desk. No voicemail this morning, and no emails to answer, so I sipped coffee and nibbled the fresh croissant. As I did so, I reflected on my conversation with Sean at the bakery. Did I commit to volunteering? *Mm, no, I thought I just said I would check my calendar.* So I opened the phone app. Just as I suspected, I had lots of free time ahead. Why not make that call? As I began to look up the phone number of the shelter, the office desk phone rang, brashly interrupting my mission. I put down my cell and grabbed the landline's receiver.

"Highland Church," I said.

"Good morning, Abbey! How are you?"

I recognized the voice to be that of the church organist, Carol Decker. Odd for her to be calling me on a Monday, the day after the Sunday service. "Good morning, Carol, what can I do for you?"

"Just a quick question. I'll be dropping off new music tonight for Mr. Milton's memorial service on Saturday. Would you be able to type up the words only for the visitors? It was one of his favorites and the congregation will be singing it at the service. It can be an insert in the program."

"Oh, of course. I didn't know it was going to be Saturday. I thought Friday was decided on. Why did they change it?"

Carol sighed. "It seems that one of his sons couldn't make it any earlier than Friday night, late. So, …"

I reassured her it would be done, and then said goodbye.

I ate some more croissant and wiped my butter-covered fingers on a tissue before looking through the mail. Just like at home, I separated the important mail from the junk. Because yes, churches get junk mail, too. I placed the catalogs for choir robes (nope, we'll keep using the 40-year-old ones we have), Sunday School curriculum (we'll just use the ones from last year), and new hymnals (we like the ones we use that contain traditional favorites), into a heap on the corner of the desk to put in a drawer later. The credit card offer for Rev. Christine Cameron I took over to the portable shredder, along with the one to "Current Resident" for life insurance. Correspondence to the pastor from the regional church office looked to be important, so that one I placed in a separate spot on the desk, destined for her own desk in the study later.

The final piece of mail was addressed to Church Secretary (Me!) and the sender stated that he wanted to buy my house. Now this was odd, because the address was the church's, and it's not a residence. Unless you want to be spiritual about it and say God resides here. And I really didn't think the church was in the market. However, it got me thinking about the several letters I had received over the past few months from a couple of people or businesses who wanted to buy my house.

I had won some money in a lottery scratch off several years ago and was able to buy a house in the quaint Summerhaven neighborhood. My home is what the real estate agent called a bungalow. It is two stories, is wider than its depth, with a huge front porch that I like to call my "veranda." A popular style and built in 1918, it was painted a peaceful Adirondack blue with white trim. In my mind, I refer to my home on Penny Lane as my happy place. The sunroom off the back allows me to view the impressive lake all year long. It really was no surprise people wanted to buy it.

I studied the letter addressed to me. It actually had my name on it, added to the church secretary moniker. That in itself wasn't too odd, because it was no secret I was the church secretary, but to have it on a proposal to purchase my house was. Maybe the company mixed up their address databases. Lord knows weird stuff happens these days with technical records. I looked at the sender's name and address. No address, but the sender, Jon Price, was one I hadn't seen before. Or had I? It did sound familiar, but I couldn't place it. Was it a name that had appeared on a previous request to buy which I had received at home? I would need to check tonight.

With nothing immediately pressing to do in the office, I decided to explore the Internet's vast array of resources regarding companies that were into buying up houses in the Rochester area. I typed "I want to buy your house" into the search engine and was pleased to see an article about the legendary "I want to buy your house" letter. Okay, this looked to be right up my alley. I was correct in guessing the letters are very common, but I didn't know that some businesses are legit while others can be a bad choice. And not only do these people send regular mail, but they can even come to your door! Huh. I had trouble believing it would be a good strategy. These days, most people don't want strangers ringing their doorbell and won't even open the door to them. Count me in that party.

As I continued reading, I began to understand this very profitable way for businesses to purchase real estate, both to re-sell and rent. The author even recommended that the seller utilize a lawyer or real estate agent to help with the process. Another site posted templates of the "I want to buy your house" letter in case the reader needed help to compose it. Then a different site said the letter is not an actual proposal, but it is often used to establish an initial personal connection with the seller. Wow, this is a crazy business.

Feeling the need to stretch my legs, I picked up the letter for the pastor and headed to the study located off the main hallway opposite the sanctuary. I unlocked the multi-paned glass and wood door and stepped into a room out of the past.

On the right was an old wood burning fireplace original to the structure. No one really knows these days if it was ever used, but somehow the bats and pigeons still like it for apartment living. Occasionally, someone found a winged visitor. Usually, they were alive and have made a right mess. Not pleasant, that's for sure. I will never forget the time I walked in to find a pigeon darting around the room, frantic to escape. Yes, I did call the custodian to help with the calamity.

And I had lost count of the number of bats who managed to find their way inside.

To the left was the built-in bookcase filled with dozens of Bibles and other reference books. Every pastor in the church's history had added to the collection and left some for the next minister. There was also a small closet for ministerial robes and coats. Pastor Cameron's huge wooden desk sat in front of the bookcase, two leather armchairs in front of it. The desktop was a disaster, full of old correspondence, books, writing implements and the computer. I placed the letter on the seat of the desk's chair. Otherwise, she'd never find the new mail.

As I turned to leave, I heard the front doorbell chime. *Oh, good, company!* I quickly locked the door and hurried down the hall.

Chapter 3

Turning the button to unlock it, I opened the leaded glass vestibule door and then pushed the brass bar to the heavy wooden outside door. Standing on the cement steps in front of me was a tall man with dark wavy hair and wire-framed glasses. As I was fairly tall myself, and was standing a step above him, we were at eye level.

"Good morning," I greeted him. "How can I help you?"

The man gazed at me intently and said, "I'm looking for Abbey Quill. The church secretary."

I took a moment to let my eyes travel down and back up his smartly dressed figure before responding. "You've found her. What can I do for you?" I was not usually so blunt, but my typical church secretary welcome was a bit subdued by an intimidating vibe I was receiving from this man.

"My name is Jon Price, and I was wondering if I could talk to you about selling your home." He stood there in his blue plaid sport coat, neat light blue summer shirt, and khaki slacks with a confident look on his face. "May I come in?"

"You do realize this is my place of work, right, Mr. Price?" I replied.

His face brightened with a smile, and he said, "Oh, yes, but I've sent letters to your house, and you haven't responded. If I could have a few minutes of your time?"

I smiled back, kept my composure, and said, "I didn't reply because I'm not in the market to sell. Seems pretty straightforward to me." Then I frowned. "How did you even get my name, anyway? And how did you find out where I work?"

Unruffled, the man said, "Oh, you can find anything online. You just have to look." He lifted his small leather cross body bag. "I brought some paperwork with me that I'd be happy to go over with you." He paused. "It's getting a bit warm out here. Can we talk inside?"

With a gaze skyward, I said, "One, I am not selling my house. Two, I am at work and will not be permitting you inside." I looked him in the eye. "This is highly irregular, if you must make me say it, and a meeting with me is not happening."

"But—"

"Have a good day!" I stepped back and pulled the door closed with a solid bang. Sheesh! The nerve of some people. I looked up at one of the several security monitors and cameras the church now had installed in and around the church building. This one revealed who was outside on the front steps to anyone standing in the vestibule. I watched as Jon Price continued to stand there as if contemplating his next move. "Go on, leave," I urged him. He took a cell phone from his front pocket and punched in a number. He then moved on down the steps and out of sight of the video camera. Probably on to his next unsuspecting target.

Back in the office, I found that in my absence a couple phone messages had come in. Taking care of church business made up the rest of the day. That's not saying a lot, because I'm only there until 2:00 pm. There were no other visitors, so a quiet day. At precisely 2 o'clock I turned off lights, checked the doors, set the alarm, and started for home.

The bus I caught daily left the corner stop at 2:10. If I missed it, I would have to wait almost half an hour for the next one to take me straight up to the lake, so I tried my best to be prompt. I do own a car. A 1971 sky blue sedan with only 145,000 miles on it. It belonged to my grandmother who took incredibly good care of it. It has a 350 V8 engine, so power galore. But it's a gas guzzler, so in these days of high gasoline prices I didn't drive it much.

That afternoon, I walked straight to the bus stop, thinking of what my dinner was going to consist of. I was not one of those people who typically has little in the refrigerator. I liked to stock up on staples for the pantry and fridge. I chose a seat toward the back of the bus as I usually did, and when settled, I caught a glimpse of Jon Price sliding into a seat several rows ahead of mine. There was no mistaking the man with the bright blue plaid jacket. I thought it odd, as I didn't recall ever seeing him on this bus route before. I filed the info for later recall and busied myself with other thoughts as the bus continued up the avenue.

After some consideration, I decided on pasta for dinner. Since there was an Italian pastry shop named Farina's on the way home, it was an easy choice to make a stop on the way. Two bakeries in one day? Well, why not? I'd just hop out, grab a loaf of fresh bread and some cannoli for dessert, and catch the next bus.

When we approached the corner near the store, I pulled the wire to alert the driver that I wanted to get off and stood up. Closer to the middle door, I waited for it to open. A slight movement caught my eye to the left. Glancing over, I noticed there was Mr. Price, gathering up his leather bag and leaving his seat. *Hmm.* With a *swoosh* the door opened, and I stepped to the sidewalk. Walking quickly to the shop, I placed my hand on the door and looked back at him. He had stopped on the walk and was looking at his phone. *Are you lost, Mr. Price? I doubt it.*

The store's delectable aroma of just-baked bread enveloped me as I made my purchases and chatted with the employees who knew me well. Armed with food guaranteed to complete my evening, I exited the bakery. Jon Price was nowhere to be seen.

I moseyed over to the bus shelter and took a seat. The app on my phone showed that the next bus for the lake would be by any minute. I had spent more time in the store than I realized. But really, who can beat wasting time in a bakery? As I began to pull a piece of bread from the warm loaf to pop in my mouth, I looked up and saw the bus about to stop in front of where I was sitting. Shoving the morsel in, I jumped up and stepped quickly to the bus door, pulling the bus pass from my pocket to run through the scanner. Stuffing the small card back into my pocket, I looked up to find a seat near the back. Relaxing in a seat way at the back of the bus was none other than Jon Price.

Chapter 4

I slipped into a seat that was in a row closer to the bus driver. I sighed. This was a development I hadn't quite prepared for. Now I was sure he was tailing me. I nibbled on warm Italian bread and thought about why this Price fellow was so interested in my house.

There were several reasons my house would be a popular choice, but I had no idea in which order to place them as far as desirability. One, my home is on Lake Ontario. That in itself was a biggie. It wasn't often decent properties with great lake views came up on the market. And mine is a good one. Two, the house had been well cared for, and maintenance kept up. Three, it's in an adorable little neighborhood and residents continually beautified the area with seasonal flowers and decorations. Four, the neighborhood is relatively crime free with many longtime residents who watch out for each other. Plentiful streetlights and a regular neighborhood patrol helped.

However, the fact remained that I was just not interested in selling. As there seemed to be nothing I could do about it at the moment, I put the Jon Price event out of my mind so I could enjoy the leisurely stop and go ride through the city to my neighborhood. Easier to do now that I didn't have to focus my eyes on Price. As the bus progressed through the city, they passed the familiar landmarks on Lake Avenue. The old photo company buildings, one now occupied by a college, and the old seminary which had been divided into apartments, gave glimpses into a much different era. I always loved riding past the cemeteries, so lush and peaceful. At Pattonwood Drive, we crossed the drawbridge over the Genesee River and approached the stop nearest my home. There were other riders leaving also, so I didn't need to use the signal wire. I exited using the front door, took a few steps and stopped, looking to my right. Sure enough, there was Jon Price exiting the bus. This time he headed off in the direction of a parked car along the street. Price was barely closing the door to the silver late model sports car when it sped off and passed the stopped bus.

After the bus continued on its way, I turned left and set out to my little house, inhaling the fresh lake air as I walked. Tipping my head back, I closed my eyes and continued a few steps, enjoying the late afternoon sun bathing my face with its warmth. But I snapped my eyes open after the toe of my shoe caught on an uneven section of the old broken sidewalk and I did a quick stumble. I picked up the pace and power walked the remaining block to my bungalow.

At the front door, I shifted the bakery bag to my left hand and felt around in my right pocket for my keys. After opening the door, I reached over to the mounted mailbox on the outside of the house and flipped the lid to check inside. No mail at all today, but better than bills. I closed and locked the door behind me and walked down the hall to the kitchen on the right. I set the bread on the counter and placed the cannoli in the refrigerator. As I was washing my hands, my phone chimed an incoming text message. Locating the phone in my purse, I opened it to see that my brother Vince had sent me a short video. Aww, another one of the tabby cat along with his 110 pound mutt. In this one, the Duchess was touching massive Diesel on the nose over and over, and Diesel just rested there, oblivious. He'd captioned it with *"The Odd Couple."* Cute.

When Vince had first moved out to Wyoming many years ago, he would send me photos of the amazing landscape, especially pleased with the view of majestic Rocky Mountains from his living room window. As he traversed the state on his motorcycle, he emailed me photos of other terra firma and landmarks. Eventually, the photos became more domestic – pictures of his cat, dog, plus wild animals who found their way into his yard. The video deserved a reply, but it could wait until I put water on to boil for the pasta.

It wasn't until I had settled on the chintz loveseat in front of the television to watch the news that I finally replied to my brother. I took a moment to wind my long dark hair into a topknot and secure it with the two wood chopsticks I had left on the coffee table and I texted back: *Charming duo. Met a guy today who works at the animal shelter downtown. I may decide to volunteer there on weekends.* A few minutes went by, and the chime sounded again. Vince had responded: *Sounds good. Just don't adopt a great Dane mix like I did!* I answered back: *Nope, not happening.*

Back in the kitchen I dumped some rigatoni into the boiling water, began heating up the refrigerated homemade sauce, and sliced a piece off of what was left of the loaf of bread. While the heat was doing its thing, I took the free minutes to pour myself a glass of my latest favorite red wine, Blended Zins, to enjoy, and set out the plate and utensils on the small kitchen table. Within minutes I had a tasty carb loaded meal in front of me. My opened laptop was there, so I fired it up to use during dinner.

As I got on my social media page, I sipped the remainder of my wine and got caught up with what was happening in the life of my friends. Gosh, so much going on in people's lives made me feel almost like a hermit. For a quick chuckle I checked the otter page to see what those little rascals were up to. Simon and his buddies never failed to amuse me with their antics. I sat back in the chair with a sigh and reflected on my recent observations. I didn't want to fall into the life of a recluse, and animals really entertained me. The light bulb in my brain popped on with a jolt. Of course! Volunteer at the animal shelter! If I had been reluctant before, now I wasn't.

As expected, my Italian meal was a feast, so I was full enough not to want a cannoli just then. I placed dishes in the sink to wash later, refilled my wine glass, and went out to enjoy the lake view from my back deck.

I gave a short toast, "To you, Lake Ontario," and settled back in the wood deck chair with a deep sigh of contentment. Tomorrow I would contact Sean at the downtown shelter and offer my time. I guessed weekends would be best, but really, I could stop over on Tuesdays or Thursdays.

As if on cue, my neighbor's huge mixed-breed, Seymour, appeared, having bounded over the short boxwood hedge separating our properties. He was named after an old joke about a scantily clad woman who had lost her dog named Seymour. She walked up and down the street calling his name and asking if anyone had seen him. The punchline is a fellow says to her, "Sorry, lady, I've seen enough!" Anyway, next through the hedge, using the old gate this time, came one of Seymour's owners, Natalie.

"Hey, Abbey!" Natalie called out. She made her way up the deck steps and joined me and Seymour, who had already given me several sloppy face kisses.

I returned the greeting with a wave and said, "If you want a glass of wine, go in and help yourself."

"Ooh, thanks!" In a minute she was back on the deck and settling into another chair, already nursing the wine. "Mmm. This is good. What is it, one of your latest finds?"

"Of course." I watched for her reaction. "It's called Blended Zins from California. Like it?"

"Yeah." She gave a thoughtful pause. "Blended Zins? What's that about? Kind of an odd name for a wine, no?"

"Ah, there's always a story behind a name, you know. This winery was founded by two brothers in California who were brought up Catholic. They used several old vine zinfandels in this red, so the name is a play on words. Not "sins," but "zins."

Natalie chuckled. "Oh, perfect! I love it." She savored another taste. "So, how's things?"

I took a sip of my wine and said enigmatically, "I've made a decision."

Natalie raised her eyebrows. "Do tell."

I described my morning encounter in the bakery with Sean from the city animal services downtown. "It seems that I feel the need to be useful, and I love animals, so I'm going to jump in and volunteer." My wine glass made a loud clunk on the side table as I set it down firmly. "Yup, gonna do it," I said with a nod.

"Well, good for you!" Natalie said. "I was wondering when you were going to escape this funk you're in." She gazed placidly at the horizon.

"What funk? I'm quite happy with my life." My glass of wine found its way to my lips as if to bolster the statement.

Natalie looked at me then and said, "You know, since Colin left."

"I kicked him out! He was a leech who tried to get whatever he could from me. Enough was enough." A slight choking noise began in my throat.

Natalie laughed. "Easy, now! I actually think you're handling it very well. No one needs to be babysitting a grown adult."

"You got that right," I agreed. I settled back in my seat. "Oh, on another topic, have you received any letters recently from someone wanting to buy your house?"

Natalie gave it some thought. "No, not lately. We've been here about 15 years and have only received one offer in all that time." She paused. "It was maybe four, five years ago? Why, you have?"

I sat up straighter. "Yes, and the whole thing has me a little irritated. And suspicious. Let me tell you about it."

Chapter 5

As the sun fell lower in the sky over the lake, creating an orange and red spectacle, I regaled my neighbor with the story of Jon Price and the purchase offers for my house. I included the letters sent to me both here and at the church, Price's visit to the church, and his choice to follow me home on the bus. I must have made the tale fairly engaging because Natalie interjected "What?" "No way!" and "Get out!" throughout the conversation.

"I did some research about these companies that offer to purchase houses, but I don't really understand why they are targeting me. It just seems so odd I'm getting all this attention," I said. "From what I understand, they mostly send letters." I sent my neighbor a skeptical look. "I don't think stalking is part of their modus operandi."

Natalie's foot rubbed against the snoozing dog's back leg as she pondered my situation. She drained her wine glass and set it on the table. "I agree this is very unusual," she said. "And I sure don't have any solutions, just advice to be careful. I'd be a little afraid. Do you have security cameras or a security company?"

"No, neither one. And yes, it does frighten me a bit." I watched the late spring sky change colors for a moment. I turned to my neighbor. "What would you recommend?"

"Well, Joyce and I use security cameras that send notifications to our cell phones if there's movement at the doors. Sometimes it's just a cat or bird briefly in front of the lens, but it's really helpful when we have a delivery or a visitor." She reached down to pet Seymour, who was snoring up a storm. "And we also have motion lights. Believe it or not, we've sometimes seen kids cutting through the yard to get to the beach."

"Really!?" I hadn't thought about that. I stretched my arms up and adjusted a stick in my makeshift hairdo. "Which should I get first?"

"Well, I'd go with cameras first. You can buy them yourself and install them if you're handy or know someone who can do it for you, or you can contact a security company. The night visuals are really something amazing these days." She mentioned the names of a couple trustworthy home security companies in the area. "But don't forget old Seymour, here."

"What?"

"Seymour, the Wonder Dog."

I looked down at the huge animal resting at our feet. "Oh, I don't want a dog, Natalie."

"Abbey, you say that now, but he is probably the best crime deterrent in the house." She smiled at her beloved brute.

I gave a slight shudder – whether from the oncoming chill, or the topic of the discussion, I wasn't certain. The horizon was showing off its dark orange colors and the sun was ready to dip out of sight. I stood and extended my arms upward. "Time for me to call it a day."

Natalie rose as well, and Seymour jumped up to join her on the walk home. "Thanks for the nightcap, Abbey. And definitely look into getting security. We think we're safe in our little neighborhood up here, but criminals will find us wherever we are." With a wave she was gone.

"Copy that. Good night. And hi to Joyce!" I called after her. I picked up the glasses and strode in, and added them to the pile in the sink. As I went about washing up the evening's evidence of a satisfying meal in the hot, soapy water, I thought about the security issue. *Safety precautions: Motion lights. Security cameras. What next, an armed guard?* After finishing up with the pots, I left all the rinsed kitchenware in the drainboard and relieved the slight ache in my back with a short bend-and-stretch routine. I had entered my twenties with a toned body from years of dance and acrobatics, and I was glad that I had begun taking martial arts classes in a neighborhood training center. I did it mostly to stay in shape, but now, considering I may need to defend myself and my home, it was probably a good idea I had started lessons. With a sigh of resignation, I went and curled up on the loveseat in front of the television.

Not a consistent television viewer, I used the remote to select the local public broadcasting channel. Occasionally there would be something to pique my interest on the station, and tonight was one of those times. A documentary about the historic burglary at the Clarence Bloy Keeney Museum in New York City back in 1990 was beginning when I tuned in.

As I watched the story unfold about the nine irreplaceable pieces taken in under an hour, the audacity of the thieves astonished me. Nothing was ever recovered, and the museum would never stop searching for the lost works of art. At the end of the program there was an opportunity to help support the museum by purchasing a book about the theft. Its title was *Theft*. Oh, cool! I need that!

I ran to grab my laptop from the kitchen table and returned to the living room. Typing the website address into the search engine brought me to the home page of the museum, and I entered all the pertinent information so I could have the book delivered to me ASAP.

Did I need the book? No, but I was a self-defined bibliophile, and I gladly added to my collection if I found something unusual or classic. And if it's a mystery, even better! I bounced lightly in my seat as I happily anticipated my next delivery from one of the Big Two companies. My heart rate slowed as I made myself relax with deep breaths. I'm not sure what excited me about this book, but I loved visiting museums, and the idea that this was an unsolved real-life mystery just pushed all the buttons for me. Additionally, it brought to mind the multi-million-dollar securities robbery which occurred here in Rochester back in 1993. I had purchased the book written about that theft, too. A fabulous account of the heist, it was written by a local journalist.

Since I had my computer on, I decided to look up the security companies Natalie had suggested. I read the reviews of both companies thoroughly and bookmarked them for future reference. It would be difficult to choose between them, so I'd have to peruse the websites more closely another time. I also quickly looked at some web cameras available. Several companies interested me, but I'd have to examine them when I had time and wasn't on the verge of heading to sleep, as well. I closed my laptop and set it on the coffee table. Even though I yawned and could feel the tendrils of slumber beginning to creep into my brain, I continued to watch the next show which was about a photographer who chronicled animal life in the wilds of the African savannah.

I snuggled down into the chenille throw pillow I'd chosen from a popular home store online because its color was perfect with the loveseat. Before I knew it, I was dreaming about lions and zebras being stolen from the Rochester Museum and Science Center. I was running around the building's interior in a frenzy with a walkie talkie and a butterfly net attempting to collect them all. Mid stride I was jolted awake when Diesel and Duchess appeared in my dream, running in front of me and tripping me up. Holy cow!

I sat up, shaking off the nightmare. I turned off the television and made the rounds locking doors and turning off lights on the way to my room. I made short order of my bedtime rituals and wearily collapsed, thankful for the memory foam mattress that had been an indulgence when I bought it.

What a day. Since I didn't have to work tomorrow, I'd look at security options on the internet as well as visit the animal shelter. I fell asleep thinking about domestic animals instead of wild ones, a much safer dream option.

Chapter 6

I awoke to an overcast sky, nothing unusual in Rochester. Residents endured over 300 cloudy days a year. The lake took on a different personality on days like these. The brilliant June sun so many people continued to expect was absent, and the gray of the lake waves portended an ominous vibe. I was content as I gazed out the bedroom window at a Great Lake that was now part of my soul after living alongside it these last few years. Bright blue or muted gray, Ontario made my heart happy.

These days my exercise routine included a daily power walk in addition to my occasional martial arts training. This morning's trek took me around the neighborhood, finishing up with a cool-down on the beach and bringing me to my back door. I took the time to do a reconnaissance around the house's perimeter to see what I'd need to secure. The mullioned windows I loved in this house were plentiful, and they'd need protection from burglars. The sliding patio door would probably need a sensor, too, as well as the front door, of course. I didn't think the basement glass block windows would be treated, though, since they were nearly impenetrable.

Inside, I turned on the electric tea kettle, set out my single cup cone filter and selected my favorite morning mug, the one with Stewart Drake's "Coffee Dreams" on it. This month's favorite coffee flavor was a summer blend. I chose one of last night's cannoli for breakfast, balanced the meal on my closed laptop, and carefully made my way out to the deck.

Once settled, I looked up security cameras. My mind boggled as I read about all the makes, models, and descriptions. I was not knowledgeable enough to install them myself and would have to contact an electrician or handyman. I took a bite of the cannoli and switched my search to local home security companies. I felt more comfortable with what they offered after studying their features. They would install cameras both inside and out, window sensors, and also smoke and carbon monoxide detectors. I clicked on the contact tab and requested an appointment with the top-rated company.

Next, on to Sean and the animal shelter. I found him on the shelter's city website. The posted photo hardly did him justice, and text underneath the photo indicated his last name was Cleveland. I cooed at the picture, "You are so much more handsome in person, Sean Cleveland." Sure enough, I was right about what they would likely ask me to do – walk and socialize the animals, help run play groups, be a greeter, general clean up and more. I decided to stop in when they opened at 10:00 am. I closed my computer and went inside to get ready for the day.

Before I left the house, I noticed the security company had sent a message to my phone while I was in the shower. They had an opening for a home estimate at 1:00 pm on Thursday. I accepted it and typed the appointment into my calendar. Excellent! I grabbed my keys and walked to the garage with a spring in my step. As I drove my sedan toward downtown, I thought about how my life was being affected by shifting crime in the city. Not just affected, challenged. I gave a frustrated shake of my head and felt my hands grip the steering wheel tightly. This is living in the city. About time I got used to it.

Rochester's animal shelter building was located on a short street downtown. The building housed not only domestic animals that were turned in by city residents or picked up by the employees, but also the stables for the city's mounted patrol. The officers patrolled two at a time, and they served as crowd control at citywide events, day or night. On a day when no events were scheduled, they could be seen anywhere within the city limits, greeting residents, making school visits, and touring parks and residential neighborhoods. As I pulled into the lot I saw one of the horses was out in the exercise pen on the left, enjoying the morning and munching on something yummy, from the looks of it.

"Hey, Buddy! Good morning!" I called. The horse turned its head and looked me over. I waved. It made no effort to approach me, and I couldn't get any closer because of the double fence. Probably a good thing for everyone's protection. But with the uptick in crime, I thought the horses needed the security more. I continued to the main door of the building and went in.

The clock in the foyer showed 10:15 and the place was hopping already. One woman seated on my left was giving information about her lost pug to a staff member. With a shaky voice and furrowed brow, she handed over her identification. I felt sorry for what could very well be a heartbreaking outcome. There was a second woman at the reception desk speaking to an administrative assistant who was seated behind the glass partition. The man at the desk, not Sean I noted, handed the woman a form to complete and return. *Hmm. Another possible volunteer?* The woman left the window to sit at a table near the front door and work on the document.

I made eye contact with the staff member as he motioned me to come over. "Can I help you this morning?" he said.

I quickly read his name tag. Mark Sullivan. I smiled and answered, "Yes, hi, Mark. I met Sean Cleveland yesterday and he suggested I come see him here at the shelter. Is he in today?"

Mark's brow furrowed into a small frown. "Yes, but he's in meetings almost all day. Can I have your name and number for him to call you?"

"Oh, of course." I wondered if the disappointment showed on my face. I had been told I should never play poker. As requested, I recited my name and contact information for him. "I'd like to apply to be a volunteer."

"Oh, fantastic!" Mark's face lit up then, and he sat up a little straighter and reached for a business card from a short stack on the right-hand side of the counter. He held the small card out in front of me. "This is the name of our volunteer coordinator, Mary Beth," he said, pointing out the name at the top. "Go to the website at the bottom and submit an application." I took the card from him. "She should respond within the day, tomorrow at the latest, and she'll let you know of all the opportunities available. You'll make an appointment to come in and meet her, discuss your skills, etc."

I wondered what skills I'd need to clean cages and walk dogs, but whatever. Mark seemed to read my mind. "There's so much to help with here, really. Everything from cleaning to greeting people, to office work. You might be surprised." His face brightened with a smile.

I couldn't help chuckling. "Thanks for the confidence, Mark. Something for everyone, right?"

"You got it!" The desk phone rang right then, and he said, "Have to take this."

With a wave, I said, "Thanks again," and headed out. The place had become filled with people while I was talking with Mark. In the small waiting area, some occupied the few chairs available while others stood, waiting their turn to speak with either Mark or the intake person seated at the door. Edging my way through the group, I caught part of a conversation about a missing border collie.

The collie's owner was practically in tears as he gave an employee information about his beloved pet. Male. Black and white. Longish hair. About 22 inches tall and 40 pounds. I knew a bit about border collies because my friend Sara who had a farm in the Finger Lakes owned a couple. They herd her sheep, and are intelligent, energetic, and very athletic. When not keeping the sheep in line at home, they were excited to be in herding and agility trials. I left the building hopeful for the happy reunion of the dog and its family.

When I got to the car, I sat a few minutes and composed a message to Mary Beth Lampley, the volunteer coordinator. Keeping the message brief, I let her know that I had met Sean Cleveland, and of my desire to become a volunteer at the center. I signed off with the usual "hope to hear from you" closing and sent it off into the unknown.

As I navigated the city streets on my way back home, I thought about all those people missing their pets. Would I be able to suppress my sadness and frustration for them? Maybe the experience of doing the intake job day after day would give my thicker skin. Not too much that I couldn't show compassion, but enough to help me endure their unhappiness.

I decided to fit in a karate workout before a late lunch, so when I arrived home I changed into my gi. The baggy uniform always helped me feel as if I could face anything. Since the dojo was located in a strip mall near my bus stop, I left the sedan at home and walked over. Approaching the building, I saw the car belonging to the sensei, and the lot was nearly full with vehicles. I had forgotten there was a noon class.

Inside, I bowed with an "Osu," the courteous greeting when entering a dojo, and slipped my sandals off inside the door. I saw the class was in full action mode, so I stepped into a smaller workout room down the hall. This way I could practice punches and kicks not only to exercise but improve my technique without bothering other students. Somewhat of a loner, I appreciated having the room all to myself for a while. Sometimes other people liked to talk more than work on their skills.

I had warmed up and been practicing for almost twenty minutes when another person stepped into the room. I ignored him, as I was concentrating on the position of my foot in my roundhouse kick. After a few seconds I finished, stood at ease, and turned to him. He stayed at the back of the room, leaning against the wall, and was not wearing a uniform. This wasn't unusual for new students, which I assumed he was. Sometimes they are shy about joining others, and often don't get their gi until a few weeks into the lessons. "Good morning," I said.

"Hi," he replied. "You're pretty good." He slowly eyed me up and down, ending with a stare directly into my eyes.

I squinted in annoyance at his subtle intimidation, and I forced a brief chuckle. "Huh. Thanks, but I haven't been practicing all that long. Still have a long way to go beyond my blue belt." Something about him piqued my curiosity. "Is this your first time here?"

"Oh, no, I don't normally show up in the mornings. I work during the day, so I go to night classes."

I turned back to the mirrored wall and met his eyes in the glass. "So, day off, then?" I stretched my arms from side to side while watching him.

"You could say that."

An odd response. Was it a day off, or wasn't it? I decided then to end my session.

Abruptly, I said, "Well, have a good workout." I left the room without waiting for his response. It's not that the dojo is unsafe, but when someone or something raised the hairs on the back of my neck, I paid attention. At the front door, I slipped on my shoes, bowed, said, "Osu," and exited. In the parking lot I recognized a car. A silver, late model vehicle similar to the one Jon Price had jumped into yesterday afternoon.

Chapter 7

Though the sun sat high in the sky, it was not as hot as it could have been. It was partially concealed by clouds that hadn't dissipated from the morning. Glad for a cooler day than the mid-eighties we had been having, I walked on the path parallel to the parking lot and stopped when I noticed the familiar vehicle of a fellow karate student pulling into a parking space.

I waited as Dave Hudson, who was relatively new to the school, parked and stepped out of his metallic gray SUV. A tall fellow at 6'4", Dave had light brown hair worn in a ponytail halfway down his back. Lots of women would love thick and curly hair like Dave's. A lead singer in a local rock band, Dave had many admirers. I had never been to his shows. But that was okay. I wanted to keep my hearing for as long as possible. I appreciated his friendship. "Hey, Dave."

Dave reached into the back seat for his duffel bag and smiled over his shoulder at me. "Hey, there, Abbey! You coming or going?" He slammed the door and used his remote to lock the doors.

"Just finished a short session," I replied. I stepped closer to him. "While I was in one of the small rooms, a student came in. I'd never seen him before. No gi or anything." I gestured with my head to the silver car. "I think he might drive the car over there. Would you know him? He's about my height, short dark hair, wore a ball cap."

Dave took a moment to consider. "No, I don't think so," he said. "Of course, that description could match a lot of students." He smiled and hiked his duffel up onto his shoulder.

I sighed. "True. It's just I don't recall seeing him before, and I didn't like being alone in a room with him."

"These days it pays to listen to your gut feelings," Dave said. "If I see him inside, I'll scope him out for you. Let you know if I sense any weird vibes. I've got your number." He turned toward the front door and looked back. "Take good care then, Abbey." He gave me a peace sign and a smile, and started away.

"Bye." I sighed again. Dave was a modern-day rocker, but with a heart of "peace and love." I stood watching him stride across the lot and disappear into the dojo. My mind wandered to what he would look like shirtless with that hair flowing free, microphone in hand. *Yes, indeed.*

As I strolled out of the mall parking lot, I thought how lucky I was to live close to the mall that had so much to offer the neighborhood. Built back in the 1940's, the L-shaped strip of stores included a smallish local food market, as well as a diner, post office, credit union and drug store. If I wanted more specialized businesses, a hike over the bridge to Lake Avenue would be worth the trip.

As I walked up the street toward the marina, a car approached me, heading in the opposite direction, and I recognized another neighbor, Merilee Dash. I responded to my friend's car toot with a friendly wave. As Merilee continued on, I became aware of a revving car motor. Looking over my shoulder, I saw what appeared to be the silver car bearing down on me. In a microsecond, my brain registered another car on its tail, seeming to chase it. As I jumped out of the way and onto someone's front lawn, I was alarmed to hear two gun shots in quick succession. I dropped to the ground and flinched, hearing the bullets hit what I thought was one of the vehicles.

I laid still, hands covering my head, and listened to the vehicles race away. The squealing of brakes indicated the cars turning right, onto my own street. Petrified, I remained motionless for a minute, trying to slow down my rapid heartbeat and telling myself to breathe.

"Abbey! Are you all right?" The voice of my neighbor, emanating from above, was welcome to my ears. Merilee stooped next to me and laid a hand on my back. I hadn't heard the return of Merilee's car.

A slight moan escaped my lips. "Uhh. Yeah, I think so. Help me up?"

Merilee held my trembling hand and then helped me to a sitting position. "I've never seen such road rage up here," Merilee said. "You could have been shot!" I hugged my knees and looked up at my neighbor.

"Me, neither. I can't stop trembling." I held out my quivering hand as proof.

Merilee crouched next to me. "Come with me. I'll drive you home." She held out her hand. "No arguments. I know it's a short walk, but you're in no position to walk even that distance."

Letting out a huge breath, I silently agreed. "Thanks, Merilee, I appreciate it." I allowed my friend to guide me to my feet, and we two made our way to Merilee's car. My legs felt a bit wobbly, but otherwise I wasn't experiencing much pain. "Nothing broken, just had the wind knocked out of me, I think. And this," I said, pointing to a reddening abrasion on my forearm.

On the quick ride to my house, we discussed road rage in general and what we had just witnessed, specifically. We agreed the phenomenon had escalated in recent years all over and had seen it ourselves, but not in such an in-your-face way. Both of us had been rattled by the incident. Merilee commented, stating she had witnessed over the past few years more tailgating, honking, and yelling, and I concurred.

"It makes me wonder what the argument between the people was to intensify it into a shootout," I said. "That's criminal."

Merilee agreed. "Yes, and speeding and aggressive driving caused thousands of traffic fatalities last year alone. Those two looked as if they had had a previous confrontation." She pulled into my driveway and put the car in Park. "I hope you'll report this."

"Oh." I frowned "I didn't think of that. I suppose I should. Although, I can't identify anyone."

"But you saw the car, and my cousin who's a cop says that the only way the police know what's going on is if people tell them."

I nodded at that. "Okay, then, I will."

"Promise me you'll take a warm bath and tend to that nasty scrape on your arm."

"Of course. Heading to the tub right now," I said. "And thanks again, Merilee. Be careful out there!"

Merilee backed out of the drive, and I gave her a thumbs up before she headed on down the quiet street.

I stood on the sidewalk and looked up at my home with its classic bungalow lines and attractive exterior. I had worked hard at what real estate agents referred to as "curb appeal." I enjoyed the time dedicated to planting the flowers and shrubbery so they would turn color at the right time each season.

I loved this house, and moving was not an option. I hated that violence of any kind, even an incidence of road rage, could spoil the tranquility which neighbors and I cherished. "This house is my happy place," I said out loud, using the current popular description of a location where one felt safe and blessed. As I entered the bungalow I couldn't help wondering why the silver vehicle had been shot at. And what did it mean for my safety?

Before my bath, I called 911 to report the incident. I assured the operator that I was okay, and she told me an officer would be out to speak with me. Thanking her, I thought, *Sure, we'll see if that happens.*

I skipped lunch altogether and luxuriated in the hot bath I had promised to take. The pricey lavender foaming bubble bath was so relaxing it made me sleepy and helped me almost believe the shooting hadn't happened. But it did. I thought about the coincidences. Jon Price following me and jumping into the silver car. The same silver car showing up at the dojo. That car almost hit me, was shot at and then turned onto my street.

My eyes opened wide. *My street! Where did they go? Are they coming back? Holy cow! Am I the common denominator here?*

I felt the bath water cooling and figured it was a good time to get out. Wrapped in my thick terry cloth bathrobe, I made my way to the kitchen. Suddenly ravenous, I quickly mixed up some tuna fish salad, made a sandwich, and piled a huge mound of potato chips on a plate. I poured myself a glass of iced tea and sat at the kitchen table with my lunch/dinner.

I took the time to consider the recent events. Even if I were the focal point, I could think of nothing that could possibly link me to anything. Except... Jon Price wanted my house. I looked around, studied my home. *Now, why are you so special, hmm?*

Chapter 8

I dressed in my comfortable "stay at home" clothes and passed the rest of the day taking care of light housecleaning and yard work. A bit of a neat freak, I felt that a clean home also put the rest of my life in order. And gardening always helped me think. I knelt on the grass in front of my abundant bed of hostas and pulled unwanted weeds from the bed. I looked at the pile of accumulated debris. A couple days of rain showers last week had encouraged plant growth, and not just the hostas, either. Besides pulling the weeds, I'd have to mow the lawn again soon. But that was okay; another perk of city living was a small yard.

As I shuffled another foot alongside the flower bed, removing unwanted interlopers and listening to the call of local blue jays, I thought more about the animal shelter. The volunteer coordinator should be contacting me soon. At least that's what Mark had said. I checked the back pocket of my holey jeans and found I had left my phone in the house. I decided to finish this bed of hostas and then go see if she had called.

Before I could pick another weed, a police car came along slowly and parked in front of my house. I stood, wiped my hands on my pants, and met the officer as he sauntered up the driveway.

"Ms. Quill?"

"Yes."

"I'm Officer Garcia. I understand you reported an incident earlier today."

"Sure did." I proceeded to relate what had occurred, and he began writing.

Finally, he snapped his notebook closed. "I'm sorry this happened, but thanks for reporting it. If you have any more problems, call 311 and let them know to add to the report. Have a good day."

"Thanks, you, too."

After watching him drive away, I finished up weeding. Dropping my gardening gloves in the basket on the porch, I walked in to the kitchen and picked up my phone. Sure enough, there was a message from Mary Beth Lampley of animal services.

Hi, Abbey, this is Mary Beth, volunteer coordinator for the city animal services. Mark Sullivan told me you're interested in volunteering with us. If you're free tomorrow, Wednesday, please stop in between the hours of noon and 4:00. I'll be in my office then and will be delighted to meet with you. Thanks. Mary Beth

Outstanding! I entered the information into my calendar for the next day. I decided to drive tomorrow instead of taking the bus so I could go from church to the canter immediately after work. Feeling a grimy weariness that was gratifying rather than exhausting, I headed to the kitchen to clean up from gardening.

Refreshed and still full from lunch, I decided to enjoy the late afternoon on the deck. I poured myself a glass of wine, chose the latest mystery bestseller from the stack of books in my to-be-read pile, and sat outside to relax and appreciate the remaining few hours of daylight. Squawking gulls swooped and plunged into the lake searching for, and in some cases catching, their dinner. Watching their repetitive circling and soaring caused me to unwind to the point that my eyes began to close. I had no idea how long I had been dozing when I heard the sound of an incoming message.

Reaching for the phone, I saw my brother had texted me. *What does Vince want now?*

I opened the message app and read the text out loud. *"Retirement consists of one Sunday and six Saturdays. Too much free time. I've arranged for a house sitter for Diesel and Duchess. Flying out to see you tomorrow. Staying for a few days, will text you flight info. Pls have clean sheets on the guest bed this time."* He ended with a smiley face.

I chuckled and then I texted in return. *ALWAYS clean sheets, you weirdo! Can't wait to see you!* Vince texted back a thumbs up.

Must be nice to be retired by the age of 40. A couple years ago, my entrepreneurial brother owned a modest company that made bobble head figures. You name it, there was a bobble head for it. A large established firm offered to buy it for an astronomical amount of money, so he sold it. The bobbles are very popular, and lots of people really go in for that sort of thing. I don't collect them, but I do have the bobble he had made of me sitting prominently on a shelf in my living room. I'm a cute bobble.

I stood up and stretched, my muscles welcoming the effort. I decided I had better check on those sheets. Horrors if my guest had to make his own bed tomorrow.

Upstairs, I found the clean sheets and pillowcases in the hall closet and dropped them onto the top of the blanket chest. A quick dusting was in order, so I hurried downstairs and grabbed the dust cloth, polish, and dust mop. I boosted the bed's shine with a quick application of lemon polish and did the same to the dresser and the wooden legs of the leather chair that sat in a corner.

I took a moment to relax in the chair and succumbed to curiosity. This would be the second time Vince would make the trip to visit me in the new house since I moved in five years ago. The first time was to inform me he was thinking of selling his business. I leaned my head back, eyes closed . I hoped my compulsion to overthink and examine other people's actions wouldn't keep me from enjoying my brother's stay. Not that he would have any motive other than seeing his sister. Or would he? I opened my eyes. It didn't really matter, though. I always enjoyed Vince's company.

In cheery maid mode, I gave the floor a thorough cleaning. I took the dirty mop over to the back window to shake it outside. Setting it gently on the floor, I pushed the olive green linen curtains apart and unlocked the window facing the lake. I lifted the sash and the screen and was about to reach for the mop when a flash of red caught my eye from the far left corner of my yard.

I thrust my head out the window. "Hey! You there!" I called. I craned my neck and spotted a person running away down the beach toward properties on the west side, heading toward the marina. "Yeah, like you'd stop." Damn, just a couple seconds earlier and I'd have seen him better. I shook the mop outside, freeing all the dust bunnies, small and large, into the atmosphere. Looking down, I noticed the unfinished glass of wine I had left on the deck. Ugh. *Not gonna drink that now.*

With a satisfied glance at the room, I went downstairs and out to the deck after putting away the cleaning supplies. I emptied the old wine into the sink and refilled the glass. A bit weary, I sat in the deck chair that seemed to beckon me and took in the view once more. The gulls had toned down their cacophony a little, but I didn't feel like reading anymore. So I continued to relax, watching and listening to the calming waves rolling to the shore.

My mind went back to the person I had seen running from my yard. Interested, I rose from the chair and walked over to the area where I had seen him. Him? It could have been a woman. I hadn't seen enough of the person to identify anything, really. I just knew it was a person and not one of my neighbors' dogs.

There was still enough light to examine the yard where the trespasser had run, but I could see nothing except vague footprints where the grass had been trampled. No clues as to an identity. I couldn't even tell where he'd entered my yard. Our lawns along the lakeshore don't have fences, so the person could have started from anywhere along the coastline. I thought about what my neighbor Natalie had told me about teenagers cutting through. Probably just one of them, I thought. A burglar wouldn't be stupid enough to wear red. A light fog had begun to roll in from the lake and I shivered. Settling in for the night seemed like a good idea, so I headed inside with my glass of zinfandel.

As I sat reading, curled up on the loveseat, my phone rang. I glanced at the name of the caller. *Dave Hudson.* I answered it quickly and with anticipation.

"Hi, Dave," I said.

"Hey, Abbey, how ya doin'? I wanted to talk to you about that fellow you saw today." He paused and I heard a noise like he had set a glass down on a counter. "I don't have much for you, unfortunately."

"Well, do you think I should be worried at all?"

"Not sure. He was leaving as I walked in, and he was talking on his phone. He didn't sound too happy. I watched him in the lot, and he started shouting at whoever was on the other end. He stood near his car, the silver one like you thought, and the convo continued for a couple minutes. Then he got in the car and took off like a bat out of hell."

"Wow," I said. I sat up straight and proceeded to tell him what had happened to me on my return home after the dojo, plus my interaction with Jon Price the day before.

"That's not good, Abbey," Dave sounded concerned. "You need to keep yourself aware of your surroundings if these guys are placing themselves in your reality. If your daily activities are predictable, it can make you a target."

When I didn't respond, he continued, "You need the Higher Power to help you. Promise me you'll be careful and please meditate on the experiences you've had this week."

I assured Dave I would follow his advice.

Chapter 9

Outside, Wednesday began with warm sunshine, birds singing their hearts out, and a delightful breeze off the water. Inside, as I sat with a mug of morning coffee, I discovered Vince's text with his airline information. He was arriving at about 6:15 pm out of Jackson. I was surprised he could get a flight in one day's notice, to be honest. Did he have a friend in the airline biz? I was sure all would be revealed later over dinner. I rinsed out my coffee cup, made a to go cup for later, and proceeded to get ready for work.

Driving to the Highland Church, I had time to think over the past couple days in respect to Jon Price and associates. I was glad Vince would be here to help me make some security decisions. A sister always needs the advice of an older brother, when requested, of course. And was always happy to be asked. In fact, I think he reveled in the role.

At the bakery, I made my breakfast choices of a couple croissants, and added in some extra muffins because of my expected company. The place was buzzing, as could be expected, and poor Jane had no time to chit chat. Satisfied with my purchase, I carried the white bags to the car and drove the short distance to the church parking lot.

The building was cool and silent, and I hastened to take my sanctuary time as it was much needed that morning. I sat in my usual seat and thought about Dave's recommendation to meditate on my problems. Sitting with eyes closed, hands quiet and folded, and listening to the slow whirring of the single ceiling fan high above me, I welcomed a few moments of reflection. By the time I was done, I felt a calm that would surely get me through the day.

Downstairs in the office, I sipped coffee, nibbled a croissant, and prepared Ted Milton's funeral bulletin for Saturday, including the special hymn selected by the family. Carol had placed a copy of the words on my desk. I discovered a long time ago the typing of memorial and funeral bulletins was always a difficult part of my job. More often than not, I knew the deceased rather well. Accepting that they would no longer be greeting me either in person or on the telephone was sometimes difficult to believe.

Mr. Milton had been a faithful member of the church for many years, and I was fortunate to have known him. He also had been blessed with quite a sense of humor, and sometimes it was the NSFW variety. But that was our secret, and it didn't really bother me. He loved to amuse me with jokes about my first name. I especially liked the one that went: "I'm starting an asphalt company on Abbey Road. It will be called Ringo's Tar." We'd both laugh noisily at that, enjoying our little routine. I would sure miss Mr. Milton.

Typing and printing the bulletin, interspersed with answering phone calls and emails kept me busy through the next several hours. At 1:45 I was ready to leave, so I took the two rubber-banded stacks of bulletins with me to the pastor's study and left them on the conference table on my way out. Next on my agenda was meeting Mary Beth at the animal shelter.

Driving downtown to the shelter, my stomach rumbled, and I remembered I hadn't had lunch. Spying a hot dog cart ahead, I parked and jogged to the vendor.

"Hi!" I said in greeting. "May I have a red hot and a cola?"

"Sure thing." The man in the white apron got busy preparing my order, and in record time I had a hot dog in one hand and a can of soda in the other. You really can't beat a hot dog cart for a cheap, filling meal when you're in a rush.

I found a bench nearby and sat to eat. Observing my surroundings, I caught myself looking for Jon Price or his friend. Being aware of my safety was one thing, but I didn't like the fixated direction that my sense of self-preservation was taking me. I just wanted to relax and enjoy my lunch.

Regardless, I finished rather quickly and was soon back in my car and heading to the shelter. Entering the parking lot, I easily found an empty space. I closed the car door and took a moment to scope the lot. Since being followed, I had become careful to check out an area before nonchalantly walking away from the car. About to enter the building, the car by the door caught my eye. A silver one. I hesitated. Feeling bold, I stepped over to it and took a single photo of the license plate with my phone. I tried to shake off the feeling of a threat, turned, and somewhat wary, I entered the building.

On the surface, nothing had changed in the place. Same posters and flyers on the walls, furniture in the same place. But I could tell something was different. I heard crying from a room in the back and I felt like an intruder into someone's private grief. Then, my suspicions of a negative situation were dashed when a woman entered the foyer with a bouncing black lab on a leash. The two could not be kept apart, with the dog jumping all over the woman like it had springs on its back feet. I watched them as they left, the duo obviously elated to be reconciled. And I also saw them get into the silver car next to mine.

I sighed audibly, relief filling my body.

"Such a joy to see, isn't it?" said the employee who had accompanied them from the back. "That poor woman had been missing her baby for four days." She smiled at me.

"It certainly is," I replied. With a final look at the woman and dog driving away, I walked over to the main desk.

Mark Sullivan was on duty again, and I greeted him warmly as I approached. "Hi, Mark, good to see you. Is Mary Beth available?"

Mark smiled back and said, "Let me check." He punched in a three-digit extension in the desk set and whispered, "Your name again?"

"Abbey Quill."

"Right, right," he mumbled to himself. He waited a moment and then said. "Mary Beth, it's Mark at the front desk. Abbey Quill is here to see you." After a pause, he said, "You got it." Hanging up, he said to me, "She'll be right out. You can grab a chair over—."

"Abbey!"

I looked behind me and saw Sean Cleveland, looking as handsome as he did on Monday, this time in a light green sport coat, striding toward me with his hand outstretched. "Glad you could come down." I felt the same charge in the handshake that I did before. *Hoo, boy.*

"Would you like the grand tour?" he smiled.

"Actually, I'm here to meet with Mary Beth, the volunteer coordinator," I replied.

"Excellent! She should be along shortly, and you'll get to look around then."

As if on cue, Mary Beth appeared behind him and greeted me. "Abbey?" and extended her hand.

"Yes, hi, Mary Beth. Good to meet you," I answered.

"Same here. Thanks so much for coming in to see what we're all about!" She turned and said, "This way!"

I gave a quick wave to Sean and followed Mary Beth down the hall.

Mary Beth took her seat behind the desk, and I made myself comfortable in a cushioned office chair. With a view of the horses enjoying the sunshine next door, I listened as Mary Beth described a typical volunteer's day. Tasks were just as I had read and expected. Lots of socializing the animals, cleaning, and other jobs. "You can sign up for as many hours per day as you'd like. We just have to know of any changes at least a week ahead of time so that the admin can make up the work schedule. It's important to be able to depend on our volunteers, just as it is with paid employees."

The coordinator leaned forward and placed her elbows on her desk, clasping her hands. Her large brown eyes smiled at me as she said, "What do you think? Are you in?"

I didn't hesitate a moment. "Definitely! Sign me up."

She reached behind and took a sheet of paper from a file cabinet against the wall and handed it to me. "You can complete this and leave it with Mark at the desk on your way out." She stood. "Any idea when you can start? If you can come in for an hour or so for a brief orientation first, that would be good."

It could have been my overactive imagination, but I thought I detected a note of desperation in her voice. Maybe it was simply gratitude.

"Saturday morning?"

"Perfect! I'll see you on Saturday then." She stopped. "Oh, wait. I won't be here Saturday. Someone else will have to orient you to the building, but no matter. Anyone we have on hand can do it."

As she headed toward the door, Mary Beth turned and flashed a high wattage smile. "Thanks so much, Abbey. You're a blessing." With a wave, she disappeared.

I was reminded of something I once heard. Essentially, if we are to be truly alive, our hearts must contain love for animals. I took a pen from the black wire holder in front of me and got busy.

Chapter 10

I left the shelter after handing the boilerplate intake form to Mark. There was a space on it for any comments I wanted to make indicating where I thought I could be the most useful, but I left it blank since I figured they would place me wherever they needed help the most. I wasn't picky.

Leaving the building, I saw Sean loping down the sidewalk from the mounted patrol site. "Hey, Abbey! Wait up!" he called.

I stopped and watched him slow his stride as he came nearer. "Checking on the horses?" I asked.

"No, just shooting the bull with the officers." He tipped his head back toward the horse stable "Sometimes when I'm not busy we discuss current affairs, so to speak.," he said. "Everything go okay inside?"

His smile caused another pleasant flutter in my chest. "Sure did," I said. "I'll be back on Saturday for a brief orientation."

Sean glanced at his watch, a large gold model, I noted. "I have time now, if you want me to show you around."

"No time like the present," I responded. *Way to sound like a cliché, Abbey.* We strolled back into the building together.

"I'll take you on a short intro to the animal enclosures," he said. "This way."

I followed him down a short hall beyond the reception desk that led to the dog holding area. A small room on the left held close to eight canines. "This is where the littlest newcomers are kept," he told me. There was room enough for adopters to socialize with the dogs. "We often see pets lost reunited with their families here." He had stopped briefly while speaking and began walking again, so I had only a glimpse of the assortment of small terriers and toy breeds. "Larger dogs back here."

We passed hallway after hallway of cages filled with lonesome dogs. These large pets looked so abandoned, it made my heart ache for them. Some barked at us for attention, some reclined in a corner of their cage. Several stood and stared at us, tails wagging. "Oh." I released a drawn-out sigh. "Is this how many are usually here?"

Sean hesitated before answering. "Unfortunately, yes. You know, too many of these dogs are just left to roam on their own until someone brings them in as strays. They fill our capacity and then we simply can't take in any more." He turned to me. "Let's visit the felines."

We doubled back and he showed me where the cats were housed. The room was lined with cages three rows high, and the variety of cats was astounding. Imagine short haired, long haired, every color and pattern they come in; here they were surrounding me. As opposed to the dogs, the cats and kittens were for the most part quiet or snoozing. "Wow," I said, "this is a change from the dogs."

Sean smiled and replied, "Yeah, you should hear them at feeding time though. The term 'caterwauling' is one you don't have to look up in the dictionary." We turned down another hallway that leading us to the opposite side of the center and opened to the waiting room.

"We're closing soon, or I'd chat with you more about the range of services the RAS offers to city residents," Sean said. "Adoption isn't all we do."

I dug my car keys from my jeans pocket. "I'm thinking I'll learn about those soon enough, right?" We walked slowly to the front door together.

"Definitely." Sean pushed the glass door open and held it as I went through. "Have a good night, and it was good to see you."

"Thanks, you, too," I unlocked my car with the remote.

"Abbey! Wait."

I stopped. Sean had moved back outside and was walking toward me.

"You busy tonight? Want to grab dinner or a drink?"

"I… sure!" A smile almost made it to my lips when I remembered that I had to meet Vince from the airport. "Oh, nuts. My brother is flying in from Wyoming tonight and I have to pick him up around six. I'm really sorry."

He focused his baby blues on me. "Rain check?"

The smile reached my face then. "You got it." I watched as he went back into the building. *Was that a bounce in his step?*

Once in the driver's seat, I turned on the car and checked the clock. It was just after 3:00 pm, which meant I had a couple hours before I needed to be at the airport to pick up my brother.

Thinking Vince would be hungry when he arrived, I had to decide between cooking or eating at a restaurant. I could go grocery shopping first and cook after we returned to my house, but I decided to skip the meal prep and clean up and opted for a nice sit down meal where we would be waited on. Nothing fancy, just comfortable. There was a popular diner near the airport, so an easy choice.

Arriving home, I noticed that the sidewalk border had become home to more weeds overnight, so I slipped on my gardening gloves and cleaned up the flower bed. Standing back to admire my handiwork, I heard a car engine and looked up to see a dark blue compact sedan cruising down the street. It was proceeding slowly, as if the driver was searching for a certain house number.

After the experience yesterday, I was on alert, and I watched as the vehicle inched toward my house. Feeling brave, I stood with my arms crossed until it reached Natalie and Joyce's yard on the left. Then I deliberately began walking toward the street. By the time it reached my yard, I'd be just about at the roadside. I started wondering. *Do I know the driver? Will I be asked directions to someone's home or a local business? Will the person take off suddenly?* The answer was the last one, of course. As soon as I was a few feet from the street, the car sped off in a hurry. I watched it leave me behind in its dust, so to speak. I didn't get a license number. Nor was I able to get a good look at the driver, though I thought it to be a man. I checked my phone and saw it was high time I made my way to the airport.

As I sat ready and waiting in the convenient cell phone lot for Vince's arrival text, I thought it was a good thing he was going to be here. The blue sedan had alarmed me. It was creepy. The thought of being practically under surveillance gave me the shivers. Also, the car this afternoon was definitely one I hadn't seen before. Was it the person who had fired the shots yesterday? If so, that meant there could be three people who appeared to be interested in acquiring my home.

The text from my brother snapped me out of my contemplation. He was eager for me to come get him after the long day of flying cross country. I zoomed out of the lot and over to the terminal where he stood tall with his carry-on bag at his side. I flashed my car lights at him and he did a goofy jump and wave. I hopped out of the car and we embraced.

"Trying to embarrass me, are ya?" I greeted him.

Vince laughed loudly and hugged me tighter. "Always, Sis," he answered.

He threw his bag into the back seat and climbed in the passenger side next to me, saying, "So, what's new?"

I put the car into Drive. "Oh, just wait til you hear." I pulled into traffic and said, "You're not going to believe it."

Chapter 11

As we drove from the airport, I glanced over at Vince. "You are hungry, right?"

He grinned. "Of course. It's been a long day. And I want to know what it is I won't believe." He lowered the window to let in fresh air.

I turned left at the light onto Brooks Avenue and made the first right into the parking lot of Kirk's Bar and Grill. I found a spot in the crowded lot, looked at my brother, and smiled. "Like old home week," I said. Some things never change. The building was one story, brick, with full glass windows across the front. The sign, Kirk's Bar and Grill, stood atop it in neon tube letters several feet high. As if advertising that it had its liquor license, there was a neon martini with the word "cocktails" across it on the right. I guess the beer signage in the windows wasn't enough.

Vince held the restaurant door open for me and we were greeted by Maddy, the sixty-something year-old manager. Maddy's relatives had owned Kirk's for decades and she was the current family matriarch.

"Hi, Abbey! And Vince! Welcome!" She hugged Vince and said, "Looking good, Mister!" He hugged her in return. "Just two tonight, Abbey?" I nodded. We followed her to a window table with a view of the airport and slid into the plastic-seated booth..

She set two menus in front of us and said, "I'll bring you water. Anything else to drink?" When we both shook our heads, she nodded, indicating she'd be right back for our order.

Vince studied the room. "The old place is buzzing." He opened the large, laminated menu and looked over the top of it at me. "We will order and then you will explain what I won't believe," he stated.

I smiled in agreement and proceeded to study the specials on the menu for tonight. Nothing appealed to me, so I chose my usual, the Caesar salad, and returned the menu to the table.

Vince made his choice and laid down his menu. Maddy hustled over.

She placed the waters in front of us, took out her order pad, and asked, "What'll it be, friends?"

"I'll have the Caesar salad, and would you please save me a piece of lemon meringue pie?" I said. "Oh, and I'll take the check."

"Of course," Maddy said, and looked at Vince. "And for you?"

"I'll have a burger platter, with bacon and cheddar and some onion rings. Also, a local cream ale?"

Maddy grinned. "You got it. Be right back."

I feigned being disgusted. "How can you eat like that and stay so thin, huh?"

"Never mind me," he said. He crossed his arms and leaned forward on the table. "What gives?"

I leaned back against the booth. I was about to say something when Maddy trotted over with Vince's ale and then hurried back to the kitchen. I inhaled deeply. "It seems someone wants to buy my house."

"Hmm. Well, that isn't so unusual these days, is it?" Vince said. "There are lots of companies buying houses for cheap and then flipping them." He took a deep gulp of his hometown ale and smiled. "Could hardly wait for this, let me tell you."

"It's developed into something more, I'm afraid." I paused until I had his attention. "I'm being stalked."

Vince stopped mid-sip and put down his beer. "Stalked? Like how? What happened? Why didn't you tell me this sooner?" His voice raised and his forehead furrowed in obvious concern.

I put my hands up, palms facing him. "Hold on, please. Don't go getting all upset. It was just this week. I mean, the letters have been coming for a while, but I wasn't approached in person until Monday." I recited the events of the past couple days, ending with the car driving past my house this afternoon. "And, as you can see, I'm fine," I said. I took a sip of my water and we stared at one another for several seconds.

At that point, Maddy arrived with our dinners and set them on the table with a bang. "Oops, sorry!" she said. "We're short-handed as usual, and I've been running myself ragged." She turned on her heel and left, saying over her shoulder, "Anything else, you let me know!"

I was happy for the interruption and picked up my fork to dig in. Vince smiled his thanks at Maddy's retreating figure and selected an onion ring from the huge pile on his plate.

When she was gone, Vince took up the conversation. "Letters are one thing," he stated. "Being followed is another matter entirely." He took a massive bite of his burger and followed it with a swig of his beer. "We're gonna talk security for you."

"As a matter of fact, I have an appointment with a home security company tomorrow at one o'clock. Good thing you'll be there to help me decide what to have installed," I said. I worked on my salad. It was hard to find one better than Kirk's. When I looked up next, Vince had finished his burger and was tipping his glass to catch the last drops of ale.

"You got that right," he said, and proceeded to release a huge burp into his napkin. "Much better now, thank you." He laughed and I couldn't help joining him. "Bet you haven't heard a belch like that in a while." He turned serious. "Or have you? You seeing anyone since that last jerk?"

I chuckled. "No, I have not, and no, I am not seeing anyone presently." I finished my salad and pushed the plate away. "I'm enjoying being by myself, actually. I like it."

"You know, you could sell your place and trade the lake for the mountains. The Rockies are majestic." He grinned. "You could live near me. Lots to do. Skiing, mountain biking, hiking. You name it."

Right then Maddy stopped by our table. She placed the piece of lemon meringue pie in front of me along with the check and took the other plates away.

"Mmm," I murmured. "Want a bite?"

Vince sat back and made a show of pretending to unbutton his jeans. "Maybe if I make room…"

"Stop it!" I said in a stage whisper. "Don't embarrass me!"

He patted his firm abdomen. "How do you think I stay in such good shape? It's not all good genes, you know."

I continued eating the tangy pie and watched him. "That's right, rub it in. Some of us have a sweet tooth." I made short work of the pie and took a look at the check. After placing cash including a significant gratuity on the table, I slipped out of the booth. "Onward, brother, to the lake house!"

Chapter 12

Driving to my Summerhaven neighborhood seemed to take no time at all with Vince filling me in on his latest adventures. He was quite the outdoorsman, and he had joined a meetup group with whom to expand his activities. He participated in all the sports he had told me about and recently began attending yoga classes.

"I tell you," he said, "those yoga poses are nothing to sneeze at. A lot of people think they're easy, but holding them for several minutes at a time can be a trick." He reached into his pocket for his phone. I hadn't heard it ring, so it must have been set on vibrate. He checked a message and then returned it to his pocket.

"Who was that?" I asked in a conversational tone.

"Nobody," he replied. "Anyway,…"

I pulled into my driveway and stopped. I turned to look at him, "Nobody? That must mean it's somebody! Who is she?"

Vince opened the car door and said, "Future conversation." He stretched after getting out of the car. "Thanks for not getting one of those compact things. You'd have to call the fire department to get me out of it." He took his suitcase from the back seat and joined me, ambling up to my front door.

"Replace the Beast? Never!" I retorted. I admired my well-tended flower beds on the way to the porch, and then I saw a package sitting next to the wicker rocker. "Omigosh!" I said. "It's here already!" I ran up the steps and grabbed the brown box. I was so excited, I could hardly get the key in the lock.

"What is it?"

Inside, I tossed my keys into the ceramic Colorado Candy Company bowl on the entryway side table and placed the box and my purse on the dining room table. "It's the book! With everything going on, I forgot I had even ordered it. Turn on the light!"

As my brother flipped the wall switch and the ceiling fixture illuminated the room, I found scissors in the top sideboard drawer and rushed to open the small carton. Vince stood, watching me tear open the box.

"What did you order this time?" he said. "Another mystery?"

"No," I said, "something different – true crime!" I released the book from its confines and held it up. "*Theft.* It's about the burglary at the Clarence Bloy Keeney Museum in Manhattan." I held the navy blue, embossed, velvety covered book lovingly.

"Well, while you're busy with your book, I'll go make myself at home." When I didn't respond, he took his suitcase upstairs and did just that.

Before opening the book's pages, I made a quick stop at the kitchen sink to wash my hands, taking no chances of getting a smudge on the pages of my newest treasure. I then took the book to the living room, switched on the table lamp, and sat on the loveseat. The book's cover had a hole cut into the front which revealed a cameo of Wilson Hopper. When I opened the cover there was the picture and a quote: "Artwork was no longer safe..."

That line itself was enough to set my heart a-flutter with anticipation. I held the book carefully and turned its pages, thirty-four in all, with photos of the stolen works of art. I could see this was going to take some serious scrutiny.

Vince came down the stairs and stood in front of me. I continued to examine the book and said, "Do the accommodations meet with your approval?"

"Oh, yeah," he said. "Actually, I'm going to head on to bed if you don't mind. It's been a tiring day." I looked up at him then.

"Oh! Of course!" I stood up and gave him a hug. "So happy you're here, Vince, really."

He released me and smiled. "I'm glad you held on to that old sleigh bed of Mom and Dad's. It's like a work of art." He turned to leave. "Good night. Don't stay up too late, now. If I'm not up, wake me so I can go walking with you in the morning."

"Will do. Good night." I watched him take the steps two at a time until he was out of sight and then settled back in my seat to read further about the 1990 art heist at the Clarence Bloy Keeney Museum in New York.

As I read, I learned that two thieves dressed as security guards stole nine works of art in about 65 minutes. "Unbelievable!" I said. I continued to read more pages, mesmerized by the incident. Not being able to put the book down, I finished it in record time and then examined the pictures of the art pieces again and again.

There were actually a few I recognized from pictures I had seen elsewhere. I immediately knew Hopper's large painting "Angry Sea at Morning" with its turquoise water and jagged rocks, and also a small self-portrait. The painting by B. Rogers, titled "The Caroler," was also one I had seen before someplace. I was unfamiliar with many of the stolen works. I sat quietly and let my brain do some recollecting. The theft occurred in 1990, over thirty years ago, so I would not have remembered the crime when it occurred. However, there might have been news articles and television pieces about it, especially on anniversaries of the burglary.

I found my laptop on the kitchen table where I had left it the day before, so I fired it up and searched for the Clarence Bloy Keeney Museum art heist. As predicted, there were several articles written about the burglary, and most often they were posted on the anniversaries of the theft. The museum staff were diligent about never letting the public forget about the enormous loss. I'm sure I had read at least one of the articles in the past, but for some reason I hadn't realized the immense cost, as the book stated, to both the museum and the public.

I sat back and thought. Why was this unexpectedly so personal to me? Realistically, I am a crime aficionado, so there's that. I devour murder mysteries, thrillers, and true crime books. Maybe watching the recent special just triggered my need to delve into a new criminal whodunit. I hoped beyond hope that after all these years, someday the museum would catch the thieves, or at least they would discover what happened to the art pieces. Recover them? Probably not, but one can always pray for the best outcome.

I looked at the digital clock on my computer and saw it was almost midnight. *Morning does come early*, I thought, so I closed up shop, turned off lights, and headed to bed. A morning power walk followed by good coffee with my brother on my mind, I fell into a restful sleep.

Chapter 13

Morning found my brother already up and enjoying the lake view from the deck. He was dressed in sweats and looked ready to go. I slid open the patio door and stepped out into the sunshine. "Sleep well?" I asked.

"Sure did, Sis." He stood and did a couple ham stretches, holding first one foot, then the other. "Do you need to stretch a bit first, or are you ready to hop to it?"

"No, I warmed up already. Let's go." I locked the patio door, and we left the house by the front door, which I also locked. "This afternoon is the appointment with the security company," I said as we began our walk.

"Good," Vince replied. "Are you expecting to make a decision today?"

"Yeah. I don't see any reason to waste time with other appointments. From what I saw on their websites, they all seem to offer pretty much the same thing." I decided to change the subject. "So, who called you last night? Your Mystery Woman?"

We began our walking with long strides, and after a moment Vince spoke. "I'm looking into a new venture. The woman who called me last night is my partner. I told her I'd be visiting you for a few days." He exhaled loudly. "I was hoping she would get the hint and not bother me for a bit."

"She's a 'bother?'" I said.

Vince grimaced. "No, she's not. It's just… I needed a break from the headaches of starting a new company."

We rounded the corner near the strip mall and started toward the bridge over the river. I said, "Two questions. What's her name, and what's the new company?"

"One, her name is Chelsea Castle. I met her in a running group and we hit it off."

I smiled and said, "Oh, really?"

He gave a me sidelong glance. "Don't jump to conclusions. She has a steady boyfriend. Wouldn't surprise me if she's engaged by the time I get back to Jackson."

"Okay, and the company?" I was beginning to really feel the walk this morning. I wasn't used to talking with someone while power walking.

"I'm starting up a hemp farm. It's a growing industry, pardon the pun."

I laughed out loud. "Hemp?! Wow, that's something. What made you decide to get into hemp?" Before he could respond, I added, "Isn't that marijuana?"

"Hemp and marijuana are both cannabis, but industrial hemp contains less than 3% of THC. A farmer can cultivate it for fiber, seeds, and oil. You'd be surprised what can be made from all three."

"Huh. Like what?" I said.

"Organic products like cosmetics, some foods, like flour; lots of people eat hemp seeds every day. You can infuse coffee with it." He chuckled, "They even make toilet paper out of it. Plus, the plant matures in less than 100 days, as opposed to trees which take decades to mature. There's lots more, but you can look it up to see the benefits of the plant."

By this time, we had reached the shore of Lake Ontario known as Charlotte Beach. We slowed down to stroll along the boardwalk to the old bath house. The water absolutely sparkled in the morning sun, dancing diamonds on the water. I suggested this would be a good point at which to turn around, so we walked slowly back toward the bridge.

Passing the closed Costello's Custard stand, Vince remarked that we should come back later for a couple cones. A visit to the lake was not complete without a Costello's custard, the local frozen delicacy. I did not disagree.

"The lines are still wicked long, but so worth it," I said.

"Can't get it out west where I am," Vince said. He changed the subject. "One of the reasons I came out to see you is to ask if you would be interested in investing in my new business. No need to answer now, or while I'm here. Just think about it, and ask me any questions that come to you."

"I will certainly consider it," I said. "It intrigues me, this whole hemp thing."

"It should. Do your research and get back to me. It really is the future of agriculture in this country. You'd be a partner."

My eyes widened in surprise. "I never thought of that. Investing in a startup." After a minute I said, "Sounds right up my alley."

Vince grinned. "I hoped you might agree. Now, first one home—

Too late. I took off running!

After showering and catching up on emails, news, and other internet gems, we both were ready for an early lunch.

"What do you feel like eating, Vince?" I asked as we got into the car. "Burgers, subs, chicken?"

"It's gotta be Billy's, Abbey."

"Okay, then, here we go!" I aimed the sedan in the opposite direction from the Charlotte Pier and drove the ten minutes to the old favorite hangout on the lakeshore. Around here, if you didn't have a favorite burger hangout, something was wrong with you. We and innumerable others favored Billy's, but plenty of other people loved Joe's Ground Round which was practically next door. The two parking lots were separated by a grass median.

Vince and I stood at the main counter and ordered our meals – two cheeseburgers for him and one for me, both with a side of onion rings. To drink, I ordered my old standby, root beer, and he chose a cola. I went to get a couple little paper cups of sliced pickles for us and then to claim a booth while he waited at the counter for the order.

I looked around the joint. It had been in existence for decades, and it had the battle scars to prove it. I think it was re-painted each winter, when business was slower, but you sure couldn't tell right now at the beginning of the busy season. The walls were plastered with photos, both black and white and in color, of customers over the years. I gazed sentimentally at the photo on the far wall taken of me and my girlfriends many years ago, when we were teens. Such great memories. I never had a summer job here, but many of my friends did. I chose the sweeter venue for my summer employment, Costello's. I never regretted it.

Vince returned with our lunch and we ate with gusto. He seemed blissful, enjoying every bite. "Man, it's been way too long for these rings, Abbey," he said between mouthfuls. "Nobody makes them fresh like Billy's." He finished his drink, wiped his mouth, and said, "I'm going to get a refill. You want one?"

I shook my head no as he left the table. While he was gone, I couldn't help overhearing the conversation of the two people in the booth behind me. I had tried to tune them out, but when I heard the name "Hopper," I stopped and began to hang on every word.

"It's only eight by ten, which means it could be anywhere. Maybe in a book?" one person, a man said.

The second voice was also a man's. "Yeah, but which house? It could be in a bookcase, though." He added, "Rick's pretty sure it's up here. We're so close."

I heard one of them take a loud slurp of his soda. "Just a piece of paper. It's gotta be in or behind something that's been there a long time. All's I know is, we have to find it before Sam does. Let's go."

Those voices sounded familiar, but I couldn't place them. Where had I heard them recently?

"Earth to Abbey!" Vince had returned with his drink, attempting to get my attention. "What's the matter?"

I whispered, "There are two man behind me, talking about a Hopper art piece. One of them sounds familiar, but I can't for the life of me remember where I heard him."

Vince stood and looked over the back of the booth. "No one there now," he said.

I left the booth and rushed to the window. I watched as the two men slammed the doors of the familiar silver car and pulled out of the parking space. "That's them!" I called to Vince, who strode over next to me.

"Are you certain?" He strained his neck to get a better look.

"Definitely. I recognize Jon Price from Monday, and his buddy at the dojo on Tuesday."

Back at the table, I tried to make sense of what I had heard. "So, these two are searching for a Hopper piece of art that is six by eight, most likely inches, and it can fit in a book."

"And what does it have to do with you, exactly?" Vince said. "I'm confused."

"I don't know yet," I said, and looked at my phone. "But we have to get home because the appointment with the security company is in half an hour."

Chapter 14

I answered the door precisely at 1:02 pm and met John Mathers, representative of the security company. He looked to be in his forties with graying black hair in a short afro style, and wore a dark blue sport coat. We introduced ourselves and I invited him to have a seat in the living room. Vince joined us then, and I made the introductions.

John asked me, "Are you having a specific problem, or are you interested in general security? Any certain product?"

"Well, I know I want cameras, both inside and out. But I guess I want general security." I couldn't help chuckling. "Sounds kind of vague, doesn't it?"

John smiled. "Yes, but don't worry. Everybody comes at home security in just about that way." He took out a notebook and pen from his briefcase. "Let's take a look around, shall we?"

He walked all through the house, making notes about windows and doors. We followed him quietly, and I answered the few questions he had. Outside, he did the same thing. Finally, he suggested we go back inside where he could show us his company's products.

At the dining room table, he proceeded to outline his plan for the house. Windows and doors would all be alarmed, and he showed me examples of the mechanics and the keypads. Finally, he quoted prices.

I looked at Vince uncertainly. "What do you think?"

"24/7 monitoring, real-time surveillance with your phone and laptop, motion sensors. It all looks good to me," he said. "This is very close to what I have in my house."

"Plus, the monthly payment is within my budget," I said. I paused to think. "How soon can it be installed? You see, I seem to have a couple stalkers. They know where I live and work."

John's eyes widened. "Well, now, I was going to say a couple weeks, but this is certainly a concern." He consulted the schedule on his laptop. "We could do it next Monday afternoon, but the rush would be an extra charge." He quoted me a price.

"Do it," Vince said. "Before I leave, I want to know that you're going to be safe here."

So, I signed all the paperwork and finalized the transaction. After John had left, I began to feel better.

"I feel as if a weight has been lifted already," I said to Vince. "Monday afternoon can't come soon enough." I stood and looked out the front window. "Anyway, I have nothing planned for the rest of today. Is there something you wanted to do on this trip?"

"Can we go to the cemetery to see Mom and Dad's graves?"

I nodded, feeling a sense of connection. I understood that I could visit whenever I wanted, but he could not. "I'll get my keys."

The drive to the historic Mt. Elysian Cemetery in the city took us down St. Paul Street into the city proper and then onto the avenue to the cemetery. A magnificent Victorian cemetery consisting of 196 hilly acres, Mt. Elysian is the resting place of an amazing number of notable citizens, important to Rochester and the world.

After a quick stop at a local florist to purchase a rose, we entered the cemetery through the North Entrance gates and drove through the gorgeous acreage to where our parents, Anna and Gordon Quill lay in eternal rest. When they passed together in an auto accident about ten years ago, Vince and I pooled our resources to provide them with a fitting headstone. My father had been a musician, and my mother a horticulturist. So, the images carved into the black granite stone were musical notes for Dad, and an evening primrose for Mom. We found the gravesite easily on Forest Avenue, one of several short lanes in the park-like setting.

Vince placed the rose and stood reverently in front of the headstone while I stayed back and let him have his time alone with Anna and Gordon.

I would often come here to walk, and I became familiar with the streets and the names of the cemetery's current "residents." As old as it is, Elysian still had burials regularly. And they took place in every season. The change of seasons in Rochester made touring the cemetery a joy. It was a wonderland in the winter, a joy in the spring, a respite from summer's heat, and a glorious show of fall colors in autumn. You just couldn't beat its outdoor splendor.

I turned and saw that Vince had finished his alone time with our parents, and I offered up the suggestion of dinner. "Would you like dinner at home tonight?" I asked. "We could stop at the store first."

"Hmm," Vince said. He closed his eyes in consideration of the idea. When he opened them they were bright with anticipation. "How about a trip to Waterman's?"

"You got it!" We climbed into the car and made the huge grocery store our next destination.

Waterman's had been a Rochester fixture for decades. They had only recently begun branching out to cities and towns outside the area, so it became one of the go-to stores when people visited the city. If you couldn't find it at Waterman's, you didn't need it.

We spent the better part of an hour strolling the store aisles, picking up food for not only tonight's dinner, but lots of other meals, too. It was hard to resist the well-stocked shelves. The dessert counter was the show stopper, though.

Waterman's bakery was well known for its wide array of desserts and baked goods. We picked up bagels and cream cheese for breakfast, and chocolate cake for after the chicken wings. I reminded Vince that we needed vanilla ice cream to go with the cake, so we traipsed back to the frozen foods aisle before making our way to the checkouts. Meals were beginning to look good at Chez Quill.

Arriving at home, I parked in my garage, figuring we were home for the night. In the kitchen Vince and I put away all the food except what we had planned to eat for dinner. I gave the wings a quick heat up in the microwave, just to take any chill off them, and put the other food on the small kitchen table. Vince put out the place settings.

He opened the refrigerator door and held up a beer. "Want one?"

"Definitely," I said.

We sat companionably at the table, enjoying the chicken and sides and casual conversation. "Sorry I didn't get a chance to buy you some ale before you got here," I said to my brother.

"Don't worry about it. I did make my plans on the spur of the moment."

"True," I agreed. "Tomorrow, I have to work mainly to take care of the Sunday bulletin. It shouldn't take me all day," I said. "If you want to use the car, you can drop me off at church and pick me up at two o'clock."

"Great," Vince said. "I'd like to see a couple friends while I'm here, so I'll make plans with them for an early lunch tomorrow."

"Who are you planning to see?"

"I contacted Tom McCoy and Brad Fraser before I left home, so they know I'm here already. They said they'd be available whenever, so their schedules must be pretty flexible."

The two of us ate in silence for several minutes.

I sat back in my chair. "Oof, I think I've had enough." I stood and took our plates and tableware to the sink. Vince gathered up the side dishes.

"Can I help you with the dishes?" Vince asked.

"Nah, I got it," I said. "You go relax on the deck."

"You don't have to tell me twice. Do you have any whiskey?"

I nodded at the cupboard near the back door. "Top shelf. It's left over from when you were here last."

He opened the door and reached for the almost full bottle. "Hah! Good thing it only gets better with age." He found one of the crystal old fashioned glasses and poured himself two fingers worth. He turned toward the patio door. "See ya out there!"

I made short work of the few dishes and leftovers and grabbed my phone before joining Vince on the deck.

He held up his glass. "None for you?"

Relaxed, I said, "No, the beer was enough. Besides, I want dessert later."

"Ahh, yes, "he murmured. "Chocolate cake and ice cream. Forgot about that."

"I'm going to check my emails."

Vince picked up his phone, too. "News for me."

We were quiet for a few minutes, each of us delving into what we deemed important to us on the internet. Suddenly, Vince sat up straight. "Abbey, you need to check this out. Go to the local news. There was a break in last night here in your neighborhood!"

Chapter 15

"What?!" I immediately looked up the app of a local news station and found the posted article.

"Looks like you're getting security installed just in the nick of time," Vince commented.

I skimmed the article. "It says the owner didn't think anything was taken, but the place was ransacked." I peered closer. "No address, but I recognize the house." I looked at Vince. "It's that way," I said, nodding to the right. "Just a couple houses over. I really don't like this," I said.

I thought back to the conversation I overheard at Vic's that afternoon. "Jon and his friend, or should I say, accomplice, mentioned they were looking for a work by Hopper. I know that name is important." I jumped up and ran to the living room to retrieve *Theft*, the book about the Clarence Bloy Keeney Museum burglary, and brought it back with me.

"Fill me in," Vince said. "What are you thinking?"

I took a deep breath. "Okay, I'm trying to remember everything they discussed." I began counting on my fingers. "One, they're looking for a Hopper. Two, it's a piece of paper measuring about eight by ten inches. Three, they're looking in houses, and thinking it may possibly be hidden in a book, therefore they need to check bookcases. Or it could fit behind something since it's flat. Four, there's someone named Sam who is also looking for it. He must be their rival. Oh, and they mentioned a fellow named Rick who told them to come to Rochester to look for it." I watched the undulating lake waves for a moment. "That's all I can remember." I thumbed through the book and found the back page where the stolen objects were listed. I read the descriptions of each one.

"Vince! Listen to this!" I paraphrased from the book. "Listed here is an Edward Hopper called 'View to the Sea.' It was done in 1929, watercolor, 8 1/8 x 9 1/8 inches. It must be what they're looking for!"

He leaned forward. "Are you sure? Are there any other pieces with the same dimensions?"

I scanned the page. "No, it's the only Hopper close to those measurements. There are two larger and one smaller in size."

Vince stood. "Do you know those neighbors whose house was broken in to?"

"No, why?"

"Time to get introduced."

We walked down the street to the house I had identified from the news report as the one that had been broken into. Like my own home, it was a cute little bungalow style building. This one was painted a bright yellow with white trim, and it had tons of flowers surrounding the house and bordering the driveway. It was beautiful, but it was much more than I could ever hope to keep up. I reached over and pushed the doorbell.

In a few moments, a tall woman with snow-white hair in a modern pageboy cut opened the heavy wooden door. Her face had a set to the jaw as she looked at us from behind the aluminum storm door, arms crossed over her chest. "Can I help you?" she said, in a flat tone of voice.

"Hi, I'm Abbey Quill from a couple houses down the road. This is my brother, Vince. I read in the news that your house was broken into yesterday. I'm so sorry." I kept eye contact with her and continued, "I think my home could be next."

She tilted her head, considering my statement. "Yes, our home was violated. Why do you think you're next if I may ask?"

I decided to be frank. "May we come in and talk to you? Or, at least sit down outside? I have some questions I'd like to ask you."

After a beat, she unlocked the door. "Come on in. I'm Julia Carlo. It's a pleasure to meet you."

We followed her into the house, which was a mirror image of mine, blueprint wise. Our decorating preferences were poles apart, although I did like her contemporary designs. Black and white dominated her artistic style, with bright colored accents to add contrast. I looked around and admired her embellishments. Any items disturbed by the break in had been lovingly restored to their places.

"I love your art deco style," I said.

"Thank you," she said curtly. "And I've admired the classic vehicle you drive." She allowed herself a tight smile.

Evidently I wasn't as anonymous to my neighbors as I had thought.

She sat in her modern black leather swivel rocker while Vince and I sat facing her on the gray upholstered sofa. "You had questions for me?"

I cleared my throat. "Yes. Have you by any chance been receiving inquiries from businesses or people who want to purchase your home?"

At this she said nothing but gave a slight nod. I glanced at Vince. "Well, I have, too. I've received several, and I was actually followed a couple times."

Julia's mouth opened slightly and she blinked at me slowly. "I can't believe it. It happened to me, too! I would never sell this house. I told that to the police when they were here. I don't know if they made any connections, but it's been a bit unnerving for me lately."

"How do you mean?" Vince said.

"Well, in addition to the letters, I noticed a small silver sedan following me on my morning walks. It also has been parked down the street a couple times."

I took the opportunity to describe what I had experienced earlier in the week. When I finished, I brought up the topic of the museum theft. I described the book and the articles that had been stolen in 1990. "I really think these men are looking for this drawing in our neighborhood. I have no idea who they really are, just the names I mentioned." I took a breath and asked, "Do you mind my asking how they got in?"

"They entered through the unlocked garage door. The side utility one, not the one for the cars. I guess I neglected to lock it after I had been working in the yard. And I never forget! I don't know, it must have just slipped my mind. And then, I hardly ever lock the door into the kitchen,"

"I'll bet they had been casing your house for a while, Julia," Vince said.

A thought occurred to me. "Julia, how long have you owned this house?"

"Oh, we bought it about twelve years ago. My husband has since passed on, so I'm now here alone."

"When you moved in, had all the previous owners' belongings been cleared out? Was there anything left?" I asked.

"Let me see." She thought a minute. "There was a pile of trash on the cellar floor that irked me no end," she said. "They should have gotten rid of it. There was also a beat up chair in the attic. Other than that, no, it was clean as a whistle."

"Well," I can't think of anything else. Thanks for your time, Julia. And it was a pleasure meeting you."

"Of course. Though, I'm not sure if I've helped any. I certainly hope you don't get burgled." We stood, and Julia walked with us to the front door. "Thanks for stopping by, Abbey. Don't be a stranger, now."

Chapter 16

Vince and I were quiet on our walk home, both deep in our own thoughts. The evening had become cooler, and a stirring breeze made me wish I had been wearing long sleeves. Once we were back home and relaxing in the living room my brother asked me, "What made you question Julia about the things left over from her house's previous owners? That seemed to come out of nowhere."

"Well," I said, "I've been thinking a lot about the connection between me, the art theft, the burglars…" I shifted in my seat and looked up at the ceiling. "Assuming this house is on their list of where the art could be, and I'm the next target, where in the house could the Hopper be hidden?"

"But—"

I held up my hand. "When I bought this house and moved in, the previous owners, the Porters, who had built the house, left a lot of stuff. Nice stuff, really. Those crystal glasses you used for the whiskey? I didn't buy those. They were left here."

"So," Vince said. "There were furnishings and other things, like, knickknacks?"

I nodded. "I never got around to selling or disposing of most of them. They're mainly in the attic. I kept some down here to use."

"Like what? Point some out to me."

I began at the front door and gestured clockwise to locations around the room. "That blanket chest, I couldn't part with because it reminds me of the little jewelry box I was given in high school; the painting of the ocean coastline I just love because the golden colors make it feel so summery; the Chinese silk, I mean, who wouldn't want that?" I continued my study of the room. "Oh, the bookcase. It's what's referred to as a lawyer's bookcase because it has glass doors for each shelf. I think it's mahogany."

"I can see why you'd keep those pieces. They're impressive," Vince said. "Actually, I like what you've done with the place." He grinned at me. "I recognize a lot of pieces from our East Boulevard house. I'm glad you kept Mom's maple dresser. It was a favorite of hers." He reached for the TV remote. "Tomorrow afternoon, why don't we go through the house and you show me the rest of the furnishings that you kept. I really don't want to go schlepping around the attic tonight."

"Fine with me." I picked up my copy of *Theft* and proceeded to read more about the museum burglary while my brother lost himself in the latest broadcast of "American Views."

The next morning, Vince drove me to work at 8:30 and then took off to meet up with his friends. But not before stopping at the bakery for my usual. I also picked up a croissant for him, and I admonished him not to eat it in the car. Croissant flakes are murder to clean up.

After going through my morning rituals at church of sanctuary meditation (as per Dave's recommendation), mail gathering, and checking emails, I got to work on the Sunday bulletin. As on every Friday, Pastor Cameron's email included the bulletin with announcements. I carefully typed them up and sent them back for her to proofread before I made 100 copies. You know us church secretaries, we can make the darndest mistakes. I do my best, but sometimes even two pairs of eyes don't catch a typo. There is one church member who will call me on a Monday whenever she finds a mistake. But she's a sweetie, so I don't mind. My customary response is that I made the error just for her.

I laughed out loud then, recalling a particularly amusing typo on my part. I had written an announcement on the insert for the Women's Society. It was a listing of items people could donate for the church's annual collection of socks and underwear for a local clothing house. Instead of typing "undies," I had typed "nudies." And yes, it had been noticed, but thankfully by only a couple people. I guess that showed me how many of the congregation actually read the announcements.

While I waited to hear back from the pastor, I enjoyed my coffee and pastry, all the while thinking about the theft and the burglars. If I was correct, Jon Price and his friends thought the missing Hopper could be in my house. If that was the case, I needed to find it before they did. And if I did find it, what would I do with it? Contact the police first, or the museum?

I decided Vince and I would spend the afternoon inspecting the old furnishings the Porters had left when they moved. Of course, if the drawing had been in my house, hidden in a drawer or bookcase or something, the Porters could very well have taken it with them. Then our search would be for nothing.

When I next checked the emails, Pastor Cameron had returned the bulletin with a message that read, *"All okay, good to go!"* I printed 100 copies which I folded by hand. When I had completed the last one, I took them upstairs and placed them on the study's conference table next to the memorial programs for Mr. Milton. Satisfied that everything was A-okay for the weekend, I headed on back down the carpeted stairs.

My cell phone was ringing as I entered the office and I hurried to my desk where I had left it. The online ID revealed the caller as my neighbor. "Hi, Natalie. "What's up?"

"Oh, a lot!" she said. "You need to get home right now! There's big trouble!"

My thoughts immediately went to my neighbors' safety. "Are you and Joyce all right? What happened?"

Natalie took a deep breath. "Your house was broken into. The police are here now, looking around. How soon can you get here?"

I sat down hard in my chair and took in a shaky breath. "Um, Vince is out with a couple friends and has my car, but I'll call him and be home ASAP." I hung up, immediately dialed Vince's number, and filled him in on the situation. "Come get me now!" I said, and broke the connection.

I quickly locked up the office and church and waited on the front steps for Vince to show up in the Beast. He drove up not five minutes later, the brakes squealing when he stopped in front of me.

I jumped in and buckled my seat belt. I looked at him with what was, I'm sure, a crazed expression. "Home!"

We made it in record time to see several cop cars with lights flashing, parked in front of my house.

Chapter 17

As Vince and I pulled into the driveway, I saw a policeman speaking with Joyce and Natalie. He appeared to be listening intently to Joyce, who at 5'10" towered over the officer as he wrote in his notebook. Natalie saw me first, and waved me over. Seymour, looking delighted to see me, hightailed it over and escorted me to where his owners were. Vince followed on my heels.

"This is the owner, Abbey Quill," Natalie said by way of introduction. She leaned around and whispered. "Hey, Vince! How are ya?"

Vince gave her a high five and then focused his attention on the conversation between Joyce and the officer.

The officer then turned to me. "Officer Polito, Ma'am. You're the owner of this address?"

"Yes, I live here." I placed my hand on my brother's arm, pulling him closer. "This is my brother, Vince Quill. He's visiting from Wyoming."

Officer Polito nodded at Vince. To me, he said, "So, what we have here appears to be an attempted burglary. Two officers inside have already checked the perimeter. It seems the suspect gained access to your house through the back sliding door. Come with me."

Joyce, Natalie, Vince, and I followed Officer Polito to the right side of my house. We stepped up onto the deck and over to the broken door. I felt my throat constrict a little as I took in the sight. What a mess! The officer pointed to the door frame.

"Here is where he used something, probably a crowbar, to pull the door right out of its track. Pretty quick work if you know what you're doing."

Tears filled my eyes as I looked at the damage. "Oh, this is awful," I murmured. I felt Vince's arm around my shoulder. He gave me a squeeze.

"Once you get a new door installed, you can apply a shatterproof window film to it," the officer said. "You should also place a piece of wood like a dowel in the track to deter any more break-ins." He looked at me. "Are you planning to install any security?"

"Yes. As a matter of fact, a company is coming by on Monday to do that." I glanced at Natalie. "A little late, but..." She gave me a rueful smile.

"How was the break-in discovered?" I asked.

Joyce spoke up. "I let Seymour out in the yard. Instead of sniffing around like he usually does, he made a beeline over here. I thought that was weird since I knew you work on Fridays. Thought maybe he'd seen a woodchuck or something. Then, when he started barking up a storm, I came right over."

Natalie chimed in. "When she saw the damage, Joyce ran back and shouted to me. I called 911." She paused. "I wanted to go in, but Joyce reminded me there might be someone still inside, so we waited in our yard for the police. That's when I called you."

I looked up at my brother. "I need to see inside."

"Officer?" Vince said.. "Can we enter the house?"

"Sure. You'll see he didn't get far. But he was undoubtedly looking for something."

We stepped inside. Officer Polito stood next to me amid the kitchen's chaos. Drawers were pulled out, contents scattered on the floor. The refrigerator and freezer doors were open, food left where it had been dropped. My row of cookbooks had been rifled through and left hodgepodge on the counter. The collection of framed wine labels I had purchased at a local arts fair a couple years ago had been removed from the wall and placed on the table, back removed.

I turned to the officer. "You said 'he.' Do you think it could have been more than one person?" I was thinking of Jon Price and his buddy. At that point, the two officers who had been checking the inside of the house joined us.

Officer Polito introduced us to them. "Officers Crane and Moore. So, what do you think? One suspect or two?"

Officer Crane answered. "We don't know exactly when the entry occurred this morning. The only two rooms ransacked were the kitchen and dining room, and it was done thoroughly. Hard to tell how many if they started soon after you left this morning. We'll know more after we run the prints."

I inwardly cringed, thinking Vince and I would have to go and be fingerprinted for elimination purposes. I tried to peek around the officers to get a better look at my dining room, but I couldn't see anything much except a blank space on a wall where a garden watercolor had hung.

Vince said, "We left the house about 8:30. So whoever did this must have known Abbey's work schedule and figured she'd be gone until at least 2:00."

"Why do you think it was planned?" Officer Crane asked.

I sighed deeply, knowing I'd have to go through the whole home buying/stalker story again. So I did, and in detail. I included my reporting of the car chase and shots from Tuesday. While I spoke, I observed Officer Polito feverishly writing in his notebook, and the other two policemen speaking together in low voices.

Finally, Office Polito stopped scribbling and said to me, "Let's look around and you can tell me if anything's been taken. We'll start here."

I stood in the middle of the room and assessed the chaos of my formerly tidy kitchen. Despite feeling heavy with the feeling of invaded privacy, I straightened my spine and made myself take in all the evident violations. It didn't appear to me that they had stolen or broken anything beyond repair.

"I don't see anything missing here," I said at last.

"Okay, then," Officer Polito said. "Dining room next."

With trepidation, I stepped into the dining room. It looked as if a cyclone had hit it. I felt my eyes begin to burn, but I closed them, willing the tears away. When I opened them, I focused on the watercolor that had been hanging on the far wall. It was on the table, upside down, its back removed. The flower arrangement that had adorned the center of my round oak table was upended. Moving on to my china cabinet, I saw that every piece of my cut glass collection and every piece of my mother's holiday dinnerware had been moved, pushed aside. Even worse, every single copy of my treasured mystery collection had been pulled out and dropped on the floor. I so wanted to run over to them, but restrained myself in order to get through this ordeal.

I couldn't help thinking, *What on earth could they have done if they had more time?*

Chapter 18

After the police had gone, Natalie and Joyce joined Vince and me outside on the deck. Vince and I took the armchairs while our neighbors sat on the wood settee. Seymour laid at his owners' feet, eyes closed. The four of us had drinks of the alcoholic variety to help us collect our nerves. This afternoon's trial definitely called for something stronger than iced tea.

As my brother looked out over the water, I rested my head back and closed my eyes, sensing my neighbors' intense, sympathetic scrutiny. A weird kind of exhaustion had me thinking this whole scenario wasn't real. *What world am I living in? Is this the reality Dave had alluded to?* Joyce's voice snapped me out of my reverie.

"Natalie and I will help you clean up, Abbey. Not that we've wiped up fingerprint powder before, but I'm sure we'll do a decent job."

I opened my eyes and chuckled. "If you think I'm going to turn down *that* offer…"

Vince spoke up. "While you three are busy, I'll go pick up a pizza and beer. Our regular place okay?"

We all nodded and he rose to leave. In silence, we three watched him pass through the damaged patio door, grab my car keys from the front hall, and exit the house. I looked at my friends, and in a chorus of sighs, we stood.

"I have one spray bottle, do you have one?" I asked my neighbors.

Joyce said, "Yeah, I'll go grab it. What else do you need?"

I paused. "I have dishwashing liquid and paper towels, but another roll would be good."

"Okay, I'll be right back." She jogged home with Seymour at her heels while Natalie and I slowly made our way into my kitchen.

"Why don't you start vacuuming while I get the soapy water ready in the first bottle?" I said to Natalie. "It's in the hall closet."

"Sure thing," Natalie said, and began the first step to removing the powder traces as I added hot water to the soap in my spray bottle. While she was busy vacuuming, I leaned against the kitchen counter and waited for Joyce to return. My mind was a blank until she stepped into the room and I looked up.

I took the bottle from her and filled it with hot water. "So, what we're doing is vacuuming first, and then one of us will spray the powder with the soapy water, another will spray clean water on it, and then we use the paper towels to wipe it up."

Joyce looked at me skeptically. "You seem to know an awful lot about cleaning up fingerprint powder. Just saying."

"Comes from reading too many mysteries, I guess," I shrugged.

When Natalie was finished in the kitchen, Joyce and I worked on the washing operation and then moved on to the dining room. Natalie had been able to remove a lot of the powder, but it was tricky to get rid of what was on the books. I found a chamois cloth in my cleaning tools to wipe off more of the dry powder. When Vince returned with dinner, he found us collapsed from fatigue in the living room.

"Come and get it!" He dropped the pizza carton and six pack of beer on the kitchen table and then grabbed plates and napkins from the counter. He gave the kitchen and dining room a glance before joining us in the living room. "It looks good. You deserve this pizza. Come on, ladies."

We took our plates and beers to the dining room where all four of us could easily fit around the table. Deciding I'd had enough talk about the break-in, I said to Vince, "Tell them about your new company."

Joyce and Natalie looked at Vince with interest. They said at the same time, "New company?"

Vince stopped inhaling his slice and took a swig of beer. "Yeah," he said. "I'm starting up a hemp farm."

Joyce set her drink down on the table. "No kidding! How cool!"

"I've been reading about hemp online," Natalie chimed in. "It's like a miracle plant. You can make all kinds of things from it." She leaned forward in her seat. "Tell us more."

Vince spent the next fifteen minutes describing his future enterprise, including where he was planning to build and all the benefits of the hemp products. While he expounded on his new project, I sat back in my chair and closed my eyes, resting for a few moments. What a day this had been. It had begun as a typical work day but ended up as something out of a crime novel. I pushed my plate out of the way and placed my elbows on the table, massaging my temples with my fingers.

The conversation stopped and once again, I sensed my guests looking at me as they had earlier out on the deck.

"If you don't need us anymore, Abbey, Joyce and I will head on home," Natalie said.

I looked up slowly. Giving them a slight smile, I said, "You two are the best neighbors. Thanks for all your help today. I'm sorry. I'm feeling drained."

"Totally understandable, my friend," Joyce said. She and Natalie rose. "We'll check in with you tomorrow."

I stood and gave each woman a brief hug. "Again, appreciated. And give Seymour a hug from me, too. If it hadn't been for him…"

"Oh, we know," Natalie said. "That dog is worth his weight in gold." With a wave, they went off into the night.

I sat back down. Vince asked, "So what are our plans for tomorrow?"

"Well," I said. "At 10:00 I have an appointment at animal services for an introduction to the ins and outs of the place. After all this, though, I'm going to text Mary Beth and reschedule it for next week. I want to concentrate on the burglary."

"Let's do some sleuthing of our own around the house, then," Vince said. "It looks as if the burglar was pretty thorough here and in the kitchen."

"Sounds like a plan." I picked up our plates and napkins while Vince collected the beer bottles. "Just leave everything for tomorrow," I said. "I'm calling it a day." He gave me a brief comforting hug. I backed away, whispered "Thank you," and went upstairs to draw a hot bath.

Chapter 19

I had texted Mary Beth Lampley on Friday night that I would be unable to keep my appointment on Saturday. I found her response in the morning. She'd see me next week, no problem. So, after breakfast and cleanup were finished, Vince and I sat at the kitchen table to plan our day of what I referred to as "tear apart the house."

I opened *Theft* to the page describing the Wilson Hopper watercolor I was sure we should be looking for. I turned the book toward my brother. "This is it." I said.

The page I showed him revealed the artwork in muted shades with the title and description beneath it. "View to the Sea, 1929." Vince said. He read the words describing the small painting silently and then looked up at me, eyebrows raised. "We're looking for a piece of paper that's only six by eight?" he said.

"I told you the other day," I said. "It's not a huge painting in a frame."

He sat back in his chair. "So, that's why the burglar is looking through books, drawers, backs of paintings. Its size makes it easy to conceal just about anywhere, and in anything. Well, considering he, or they, have done a pretty good job in here and the dining room, where else do you want to start?"

"I've thought about it, and since the attic is so dusty, let's do it last. No reason to get all dirty if we don't have to. First the library, then the living room, and finish up upstairs." I pushed myself up from my chair. "Ready?"

Vince and I spent the next several hours going through the first floor of the bungalow with a fine-tooth comb. We looked under, between, in back, in front, and every other place we could investigate. With a short break for lunch, aka leftover pizza, all the rooms on the main floor and second floor had been examined by mid-afternoon. Unlike the burglars, we put everything back in its proper place.

In the guest room I said, "I know it's weird, but realizing that a burglar has been in my home makes me feel as if we've been watched all day."

Vince laughed. "Really, Abbey? It's not like they can climb a tree and stare in your windows."

"What?" I ran to the window overlooking the back yard, where I had seen the trespasser a few days ago. "I have a couple large trees. They could do just that!" I eyed a huge sugar maple with distrust.

"Come on," Vince said. "Do you want another break, or shall we head on up to the attic?"

Shaking myself out of the brief distraction, I joined my brother at the door. "Up we go."

"Do we need flashlights?" he asked as we walked down the hallway.

"No, I installed two fluorescent lights a couple years ago. They're like shop lights, but they're connected to the stairwell fixture." I flipped a wall switch before opening the attic door, and the stairway was lit up for us by a small glass ceiling light. Vince followed me up the short flight of stairs to the attic. It's look was so typical of old houses.

Unlike some homes, my attic had never been renovated to be used as another room. Instead, you can see the plywood under the roofing shingles, and the floor was the original 2"x4" planks. The previous owners had installed a window fan. When I left the attic door open it moved the hot air from downstairs during the summer. I didn't need air conditioning most of the time.

Vince moved down the center of the attic, turning on the lights as he went. The dusky, dim storage space was revealed in all its glory. My penchant for neatness extended even here, as he noted. "Sheesh, you could live up here if you wanted to. Have you thought about making it into another bedroom?"

"But where would I put all my stuff?" I said. "The basement is too damp, even with the dehumidifier."

"Yeah, there's that," he agreed. "So where do you want to start? You take one end, I take the other?"

"No need. It's all over here." I walked to the north side of the attic, and Vince followed me.

"Pretty nice pieces up here," he commented, looking over my shoulder at the furnishings which had once been used by another family.

"I never thought that separating my stuff from the previous owners' would be helpful in this particular way," I said. "When I moved in, I just pushed all their leftover junk to this side. Lots of it is quite pretty, though," I said, as I looked it over. "I'll bet someone who ran a bed and breakfast would really like to decorate their place with it."

"Good point," Vince said, as he opened drawers of an old dry sink that was probably made of cherry. "None of this seems any newer than early nineteen hundreds." As he pulled out each drawer, he checked underneath to be sure there was nothing attached.

As he explored the larger furniture, I found a stack of paintings and prints in a large cardboard box, one of three placed on the floor. I pulled close to me an upholstered slipper chair which had seen better days and sat to work on the pictures. The first box held mainly prints of famous artists, such as Monet, Van Gogh and Rembrandt. There were a few black and white etchings of coastal scenes which I thought I might actually want to hang downstairs.

I moved the box away from me and dragged the next one over. I glanced at Vince and saw he had finished going through the dry sink, the oak commode with two drawers and a set of doors, and was now admiring a glass door bookcase. I sat up in the chair and stretched. His phone rang, startling us both.

"Huh. Good connection up here," he said, and he pulled his phone out of his jeans pocket. "I have to take this. It's Chelsea."

Remembering that Chelsea was his new business partner, I rose from my chair. "Let's call it a day, then. I'm getting tired."

Vince nodded as he answered the call. I left him speaking on the phone, and walked down the stairs to the second floor. When he joined me, I closed the door and hit the wall switch. He went on to the guest room, continuing to speak with Chelsea, and I headed downstairs to the kitchen. Seeing the time, I realized we had been working for hours longer than I thought we had. And it was time to think about dinner.

I started a pot of rice in the cooker and then sliced chicken breasts into bite sized pieces. Then I fried up the chicken, added chopped asparagus, pepper, onion, and carrots, and then the rice was just about ready. As I added the splash of soy sauce, Vince entered the kitchen and started setting the table for two.

"Homemade stir fry! Excellent!" he said. He looked in the fridge. "What do you want to drink?"

"Oh, just water tonight, I think," I said. I kept stirring the wok.

Vince chose a beer for himself and filled a glass of water from the refrigerator's dispenser for me.

"Bring the plates over and I'll fix them here." When he did, I scooped fluffy, white rice onto our plates and added the stir fry on top. I handed him his and said, "Here you are, sir."

Vince inhaled the pungent aroma deeply and practically drooled. He actually rubbed his hands together in delight after he sat down. "Wish I had someone to make this for me back home."

"Oh, for heaven's sake, Vince," I said. "It's one of the simplest dishes to make. Prep takes minutes." I swallowed the first bite, and yes, it was divine.

After devouring half his plateful, Vince said, "Eh, I'm just not a good cook."

"You know," I said. "You could take cooking lessons. Socialize, meet people." I looked up at him with a smile. "Female people, even."

He hefted his beer, stared at me, and said, "Not a bad idea, Sis. Not bad at all."

After cleaning up, we drove over to Costello's to grab a couple pistachio-pineapple cones and stroll along the pier. We discussed our strategy for the next day and decided to finish searching the attic. After that, who knew? I guess it would depend on what we found.

Chapter 20

On Sunday morning we returned to the attic after breakfast. There were still a couple boxes of paintings and prints I hadn't finished looking at, so I delved into them first. Vince began where he'd left off, the bookcase.

"That's a pretty unit," I said. "Maybe I can find some room for it downstairs."

"You sure have enough books to fill it," my brother remarked. "I'll help you move it before I leave, if you want." He had finished feeling under the shelves and examining the back and was ready to move on to a small leather-topped table.

"Great, thanks," I continued leafing through the pictures.

Vince stopped his work abruptly and looked over at me. He said, "You know, if we're looking for a single sheet, you really should be removing the backs of those frames."

"Huh?" I sat back in my chair.

He looked at me and said pointedly, "You're the mystery fan. You should know people often hide documents behind paintings."

"You're right! How could I not remember that!" I was about to continue my search with renewed vigor, but I realized I'd ruin my manicure if I continued picking at the staples. I found a screwdriver in a plastic bucket of miscellaneous tools I'd left against one wall and used it to open up the back of every print and remove the piece of cardboard. "Nothing," I muttered.

Vince had finished looking at the larger pieces of furniture and came over to help me. He sat on the bare wood floor and began assessing the third box. As he became engaged with those pictures, I returned my attention to the first box I had looked at the day before. None of the prints of the masters revealed anything, and I moved on to the black-and-white etchings of coastal scenes. The pictures were of landmarks and notable places along the eastern seaboard, five in all, each with a thin black wood frame. Included in the collection were drawings of the Cape Neddick "Nubble" Light, the Gloucester Fisherman's Memorial, the Cliff Walk in Newport, Race Point Beach in Provincetown, and the Portland Head Light in Maine. Each piece had the scene's name noted in a flowery script on the front lower left corner.

I examined them closely before opening the backs. To my untrained eye, I couldn't tell if they were etched or engraved. They could have been just reproductions, which I would have been able to detect with a simple magnifying glass. But that detail I could look into later. Surprisingly, none of the pieces was stamped with the name of the artist or frame shop. I carefully removed the back of the Cape Neddick print by pulling back on the tacks holding it to the wooden frame. My effort revealed nothing hidden behind the art, so I moved on to the next.

I proceeded to perform the same delicate ritual with three of the other drawings, and my enthusiasm and faith that I would find the stolen artwork lessened with each one. Finally, "Portland Head Light, Maine" was my last hope. I smiled a bit as I gazed at it, letting myself get lost in the past. I had visited this lighthouse once. A friend and I had made the trip to Maine and camped along the way. Every year, for one day, the coastal lighthouses are open to the public for free. It was a warm September day, and I recalled that climbing the 85 steps hadn't seemed so bad at first, but, boy, did I feel the ache afterward.

I placed the frame across my lap and bent the staples back. By this time Vince had finished looking through the box and other items left behind, and he sat on the floor next to me, legs outstretched, leaning back on his arms.. I gently lifted the cardboard back from between the staples and my breath caught in my throat. I heard a sound, like a squeal or yelp. I felt Vince staring at me.

"Abbey! What is it?" He jumped up and stood looking over my shoulder. "Holy…"

With quivering fingers, I finished separating the frame from the cardboard and handed it to Vince. There, on my lap in front of us, was a single 6" x 8" watercolor that had been concealed behind the lighthouse etching. We continued to stare at it, not believing what we were seeing. My eyes traveled to the lower right corner where I clearly read the artist's signature.

"Wilson Hopper," I whispered. "View to the Sea, 1929."

"Hopper!" my brother shouted. "Hopper!" He jumped and spun around, smacking his hand into his fist. "I don't believe this!"

My reaction was practically the opposite of Vince's. In quick, shallow breaths I murmured, "I… I don't dare touch it." I looked up at Vince. "What do I do now?"

He paced the floor with determined strides. "Okay, first, we should contact the museum. Let them arrange to authenticate it." He opened his phone and began taking photos of the artwork. "This will show how we discovered it, in case there are any questions," he said. "For now, is there a place you can hide it?"

"Yeah," I said. "The floor safe in my bedroom closet."

"A floor safe?" Vince sounded skeptical. "Are you sure it's secure enough? No one could carry the thing out?"

I stood and walked to the stairs, carefully cradling the lighthouse print and its valuable contents to my chest. "It's bolted to the floor. Grab the lights?"

The two of us headed down the stairs to my room. I handed the pieces to Vince and knelt to open the safe where I kept important papers like my passport and my will. The frame fit snugly with little wiggle room, and I closed and locked the safe. I stood. "Let me get *Theft*, and I can look up the contact numbers that are listed in it."

In the living room, I picked up the book and paged through it, searching for the telephone numbers. "Hmm," I said. "Not here." I thought a moment. "Oh, I must have seen them on the museum website!"

I replaced the book on the coffee table and grabbed my laptop. Sitting on the loveseat, I opened a search engine and typed in the museum's name. On the website, I found the page listing the numbers. "Here it is."

Vince sat next to me. "Where's your phone?"

"Um," I frowned. *Where did I leave it?* The memory of the break-in made my heart pound. "Check the kitchen for me?"

He found my cell phone on the table where I had been using it at breakfast and brought it over. "Here you go."

With shaky hands, I typed in the phone number to the New York museum. I sat impatiently, listening to the recording. Hanging up, I said, "No live person. The message said they're open, but I can't even leave a message. What's the number of the security person?"

Vince pointed out the contact number on the computer screen for the head of the theft detail, and I tried that one. Still no live person, but I was able to leave a message. I stated my name, number, and a short message for them to please call me regarding an urgent matter. I repeated it, and then hung up.

"What do we do in the meantime?" I said. "Call the police?"

"We could," Vince said. "But I don't think you'll get any action from a phone call, and an in-person visit might be your best chance of immediate action. You know, this whole discovery has me wound up. I really want to clear my head. Besides, I'm getting hungry." He stood and walked around the room. "Why don't we go get something to eat and then go to the local police station? We might get a call from the museum in the meantime."

While my brother had an appetite, this whole experience left me feeling gutted. Yet I felt euphoric at the same time. "I have a bad feeling about leaving the house, Vince. Why don't you go and get take out for us?" I implored.

My brother placed his hands on my shoulders in a comforting gesture. "The painting is safe, Abbey. You know we need a break." I knew the drawing was in a safe place and soon we would have to disclose to the authorities that it was in our possession.

Mindful of those facts, I grabbed my keys and we drove to Billy's. Nothing like burgers and rings to help in a crisis.

Chapter 21

At Billy's, everybody and his brother had the same idea we did. The place was packed to the gills. I left Vince at the counter to order for us, filled two small paper souffle cups with sweet pickles, and grabbed a table outside. As I munched on a pickle slice, I looked out over the lake and relived the discovery of the Hopper. I watched those around me as they enjoyed their meals and the company of their families and thought, *"You have no idea what just happened in our tiny peaceful community. We found a stolen piece of art worth probably hundreds of thousands of dollars."* I closed my eyes, feeling tired, questioning the reality of the last few hours.

Vince set the tray on the table and I came back to life. In typical fashion, he had finished his burger when he noticed I wasn't eating much. I idly tasted an onion ring and took a sip of soda.

"Really, Abbey? You're not going to eat?" His face registered a combination of worry and disbelief.

"I can't help it, Vince." I covered my face with my hands. "This is incredible."

"I know," he said, voice full of concern. "When have you ever not been able to consume Billy's rings?"

I lifted my hands, mouth agape. "What?!"

He guffawed, loud enough for customers around us to hear and glance our way. "Kidding, sweetie," He reached over the table, patting my shoulder. Popping the final onion ring into his mouth, he added, "It's been a day. And it's not over yet."

I was just about to concur when my phone blasted its vintage telephone ring tone. "It's Natalie." I locked eyes with Vince. "Last time she called it was bad news." I slid the button to answer. "Hey, what's up?"

"Okay, you're not going to believe this, but Seymour caught a burglar!"

"What? Where?"

There was a slight pause. "Your house."

I shot up out of my seat like a cannonball. "Are you kidding me!" I shouted. "On my way." Vince and I left our tray on the table and took off for home.

When we arrived, the scene at my house was more hectic than it was on Friday. I lost count of the police cars as Vince and I ran through the front door and out the back. Too many people to count, police officers and neighbors alike, loitered in my yard. I stopped in my tracks and searched for an officer in charge, or at least, my neighbors, to fill me in. My eyes focused on Officer Polito who had been in charge at the break-in on Friday. He quickly strode over to meet me. "Ms. Quill," he greeted me.

"Officer Polito," I responded. "What's happened?"

"Come with me," he said. I followed him to the right side of the back yard, where two men were sitting on the lawn, their hands cuffed behind them.

"Do you know these two individuals?"

The Wilson Hopper watercolor with its bold blue sea and cliff-like brown rocks flashed before my eyes. Without responding to the officer, I took off on a run into the house and to the safe bolted to the floor of my bedroom closet. It looked untouched, but I wasn't thinking clearly, and I fumbled with the combination lock and wrenched open the heavy metal door.

When my hand brushed against the watercolor, I gently pulled it out, verifying its existence to slow my pounding heart, and locked it up again. I took my time on the way down the stairs to control my breathing and replace my panic with what I hoped was a calm demeanor.

"So sorry, Officer," I said. "Slight emergency, that's all." I gave Vince a reassuring nod.

"As I was saying," Officer Polito continued, "Do you know these two men?"

I could hardly believe what I was seeing. "I sure do! Jon Price and his friend." I corrected myself. "No, partner."

"And how do you know them?"

"I spoke to Mr. Price last week," I began in a controlled voice. "He offered to buy my house. He followed me home, and—."

Jon Price took the moment to interrupt me, shouting, "She's lying! I've never seen her before!" He struggled against the handcuffs in vain.

"And him," I said, pointing to the other man. "He approached me at the dojo last week. And I've seen him in a silver car that almost ran me down." The fellow just looked away, shook his head, and said nothing.

"So, what happened?" I felt my body tensing in anger.

"They were breaking in to your home through this window here," he said, and pointed to the shattered window to my library. "Apparently, Mr. Price broke it and climbed through, and was helping Mr. Carson in when your neighbor's dog noticed and decided they ought not to be doing that."

My eyes widened and I looked at Vince. He smiled and nodded to Seymour, who sat, thumping his tail on the ground and looking pleased with his part in the takedown. "Good boy!"

Joyce and Natalie, along with Seymour, stepped over to join our small circle. Seymour jumped up on Vince, who, having a huge dog himself, was ready for the playful assault. While the two of them wrestled, my neighbors filled me in.

"We were sitting in the kitchen when Seymour started going crazy," Joyce began. "I let him out, and just like before, he made a beeline for your house."

Natalie said, "Only this time he caught these two in the act of breaking in! Seymour bit ahold of the one guy's leg and just wouldn't let go. I watched while Joyce called the police." She grinned. "I figured if it became more than a game of tug o' war, I'd step in. It really looked like something out of *Dumb Plus Dumber*."

Price's partner, Carson, attempted to stand but fell over on his side. He yelled, "That dog attacked me! I think he drew blood! I wanna press charges!"

"Can he do that?" I asked Officer Polito.

He gave a small smile, "Sure, but it wouldn't amount to anything. He was caught in the act. Doesn't look hurt, either, just mad."

Vince left Seymour panting on the ground and said to Office Polito, "I think we need to sit down and discuss with you what has happened here today, and I don't mean just this." He nodded his head toward the two men. "I'm sure they're involved, but I'm also sure they're not going to give you an honest account of why they chose my sister's house to rob."

As extra officers who had been called to the scene began to leave, Price and Carson were hoisted to their feet by the four remaining cops and led around the side yard to waiting police vehicles. I took in the sight my diligent neighbors, Joyce and Natalie, and Seymour the wonder dog. I gave both women warm hugs and included Seymour in the love. "I appreciate you more than I can say. And especially you, Seymour," I said, kissing the top of his huge head and causing his long, natural tail to whip back and forth in a frenzy. We all laughed. "See you tomorrow," I said. Joyce and Natalie waved good night and followed our hero back home.

Officer Polito pointed his notebook toward my house. "Shall we?"

As we entered the kitchen, I turned to Vince and said, "What about the library window?"

"We'll find something to cover it for tonight and we'll pick up some board tomorrow. I'll order a window for you," Vince offered. I put my hand on his arm and smiled in gratitude. A big brother sure comes in handy.

Once seated at the kitchen table, Officer Polito opened his notebook and readied his pen. "Okay, then. Let's start at the beginning." Vince leaned forward, his arms on the table, to begin the report, and I joined the two men.

"It all started with a purchase offer in the mail," I told him. "When we're done here, I'd like to show you some very significant artwork."

Epilogue

By the end of August, the Hopper had been returned to the Clarence Bloy Keeney Museum and the two burglars had been tried and sentenced. As far as I know, the police are still looking for their ringleader, the fellow named Rick.

Officer Polito contacted he officials of the Keeney Museum. The museum director, the director of security and the director of archives all traveled to Rochester to meet with me and secure the painting. I suppose they didn't want to risk the watercolor going missing again before they had their hands on it, though I did keep it locked in my closet safe. After verifying the art and hearing my story of how it ended up in my possession, I was presented with a check in the amount of $200,000 as a finder's fee. I'm not sure if the painting was worth that much, but I was pleased with their generosity.

I read online that a major auction house in New York City was offering several Hopper pieces for sale that fall. Evidently the museum that owned them needed funds. The auction estimates were in the $150,000 - $500,000 range.

The return of the painting to the museum officials was held in my home library in front of the fireplace that has my original James Fenton oil of Cape Cod hanging above the mantel. (Maybe Fenton can become a celebrity now.) The story and photos were carried by local and national news agencies, and even world outlets. I'm just thankful they didn't want pictures in the attic where I had discovered it. I've not had a chance to look for any other treasures yet.

The Agatha Solutions

Chapter 1

It was an unusually muggy day for October. Humid enough that I opened the windows in the office to let some of the heat out. The 110-year-old church where I work as a secretary would never have air conditioning. I had asked a couple years ago, and the response from the head Trustee was, "No need for it. We just open the windows if it's too hot." And that was from a board member who was in church only on Sundays and never attended worship during the summer months.

Standing at the church window on Monday morning, I blew my dark hair out of my eyes and shook my head. Aloud I said, "I really know better than this." My problem right then wasn't the heat exactly, it was the fact that I had gotten two fingers of my right hand stuck between the window sashes. I had been attempting to cool the office by encouraging a breeze to waft in. The wood double hung windows were original to the building, and this one had only one sash cord that threatened to tear at any time. I looked at my hand and frowned. *They should have updated these windows at the same time they did the office. But, of course, that was too logical.*

Praying the phone wouldn't ring while I was "otherwise engaged," I slowly, painstakingly, used my left hand to pry apart the two frames and wiggled the fingers on my right hand to disengage them. After a couple long minutes, my hand was freed, but not without a deep scratch which looked as if it would leave a scar. "Probably deserve that," I said. I was brought out of my contemplation by the ringing of the telephone.

I massaged my throbbing fingers while walking to my desk and answered the first call of the day. "Highland Baptist Church."

"Abbey! Good morning, it's Marjorie Briscoe. How are you, dear?"

The ache in my fingers momentarily forgotten, I greeted the octogenarian with a smile in my voice. Marjorie was silver-haired senior who acted as if she were fifty years younger.

"And good morning to you, Marjorie." I walked over to check the large paper desk calendar that, as church secretary, I kept for all the Highland Baptist Church events. "I see from the calendar your women's group is starting up again this week. Do the Agathas still want to meet in the parlor?"

"Oh, yes, dear, that'll be fine. You know, we are so looking forward to our first meeting of the fall. With two of our members out sick, we hadn't wanted to begin our usual gatherings. But Helen and Ruthie are much better now, so off we go!"

I could hardly hold back a chuckle and grinned broadly at her vivacious tone. Marjorie was one in a million. *Wish I had her energy.*

"You and the ladies are penciled in for Thursday at noon. How many are you, now? I forget."

Marjorie sighed. "Well, with the passing of Carol Ann last May, we're down to five in number. I'll need to discuss with the girls how we can recruit new members." She paused. "You're always welcome to join us, Abbey. We could use new blood."

I wasn't sure how I felt about the term "new blood," considering I really didn't know just what went on in the little group of older ladies. Marjorie had encouraged me to join them in the past, but I always found a reason to shy away from attending. Maybe I should re-think my position on the matter.

"Marjorie, what is it that you women do?" I asked. "I mean, what is the group's purpose?" Even though the women were church members, they met apart from the church's Women's Society which planned fellowship activities and raised funds for various area ministries.

"Oh, my goodness. What do we do? I suppose you could say that we attempt to solve the world's problems," she said. "Really, though, at each meeting we address a certain dilemma, a quandary, you know. It can be related to anything, as long as it's a situation needing to be resolved."

"Do you come up with a solution at every meeting?"

"No, not every time, I'm afraid. But sometimes after we have had a while to think about it, one of us does come up with a result to share the next time." I could hear Marjorie's pride through the phone line. "And of course, we always have lunch! Can't enjoy a noon meeting without lunch." Marjorie giggled and continued. "We each bring our own sandwich, and one of us is volunteered to bring that day's dessert."

I laughed at her last remark. "Maybe I should come just for that reason alone. I rarely turn down dessert!"

"I'll let you get back to work now, Abbey. Thanks for your help, and please know you are welcome to join us anytime. Besides, we heard about your experience with that stolen painting. We'd love to learn more about it," Marjorie said, closing the conversation.

"My pleasure, Marjorie. Bye, now."

I replaced the receiver in its cradle and thought about the Agathas. Their meeting wouldn't cut into my work day because I'm only here in the office on Monday, Wednesday, and Friday. I accessed my phone's calendar. Tuesday and Thursday mornings I helped out at the animal shelter, so I would be able to attend the Agatha meetings. *What the heck, why not?* I entered "Agathas" on the upcoming Thursday at noon. Besides, maybe I would discover the reason behind their name.

I walked into the animal shelter Tuesday morning thinking I might say hello to Sean Cleveland, the communications director, before I started working on the computer. Several months earlier I had met Sean when he was posting flyers at the Brooks Bakery. We dated a few times, but it became obvious that our interests didn't align enough for a long-term relationship. We didn't like the same movies (me: comedy and mystery/thrillers, him: action and horror flicks), didn't enjoy the same restaurants (me: diners and Italian, him: Indian and more Indian). Even our politics didn't align. Our conversations were difficult sometimes because we didn't have a whole lot in common except the shelter. He may not have been dating material, but unexpectedly, when I needed good advice, he was a go-to friend.

My duties at the animal shelter had begun with the mundane-- cleaning cages, walking and feeding the dogs. I was gradually promoted to the job of updating the website. Not to say that I still didn't help out in other ways, but admin is more my speed. I happened to catch Sean in his office writing energetically on some document.

I gave the open door a light knock. "Morning, Sean," I said.

He looked up with his dazzling grin that could chase anyone's blues away. "Hey, Abbey, good to see you!" he said. "How's the world treating you?" He put down his pen and sat back in the chair. "Take a seat."

As I settled into a chair, he said, "I kept up with the burglary in the news for a while. Have they gone to trial yet?"

"Yes, guilty as charged and serving their time," I said. "It was pretty much an open and shut case. The circumstances of their arrest had them screaming for mercy."

He laughed. "I guess being cornered by a massive canine will do that!"

I had to chuckle, too. Looking back, it had been like a scene out of a comedy sketch.

Sean's expression turned serious. "So now you have a new normal. I'm guessing you installed the security you mentioned to me. Do you feel safer?"

I considered that. "Yes, to a point. Once your home has been violated it's really hard to stop thinking that someone is around the corner waiting to jump you. Sometimes when I walk in the front door I look around, make sure nothing's been moved." I checked my manicure and fiddled with my garnet ring.

Nodding, he asked, "Have you considered adopting a large dog from here?" I looked up. "You love these dogs, Abbey, I know you do. Think about the difference one of them can make in your life. Unconditional love from them, right?" He leaned forward on his desk. "Adopted dogs are known to bond with their rescuers. I think you'd feel safer, and you'd have another sentient being in the house to give you security and comfort."

I didn't reply right away. Sean sounded like one of the pamphlets he writes. Then again, he made a good point. But was I ready for a dog and taking care of its needs? I'd lived alone for a long time. Maybe I didn't want the responsibility.

As though sensing my thoughts, Sean said, "I'm sure you could take it with you to work. And I know you walk a lot." He smiled. "Dogs tend to like that."

I looked at him with a smirk and stood. "Yeah, I've heard that. I'll think about it. Good to see you as always, Sean." I left the room and automatically turned left toward the dog kennels.

Adopting a dog had actually been on my mind since the break-in. My neighbors had Seymour, a huge mixed breed that was a love. He also had a dark side that would show up if you proved you were not a friend. Thankfully, we were friends. But I was still bothered thinking about the work that came along with the adoption. Anyway, no harm looking.

I strolled past the small pups, knowing I'd feel safer with a larger dog that would scare off anyone inclined to crime. Similar to all neighborhoods in the city, mine had violence encroaching faster than we liked or expected. I also thought about what Sean had said about a walking partner.

The rows of cages were filled with medium and large sized dogs in a variety of mixes which resulted in a huge range of coat colors and markings. Short fur, long fur, brown, black, white and unique mixes of the above. Pit bull blends seemed to be the flavor of the day. Unfortunately, too many have been bred, and those dogs that were no longer wanted filled the majority of the pens. By the time I had finished studying all the building's "guests," my brain was tired. No one would be going home with me today.

Chapter 2

Thursday morning I was once again at the animal shelter seated in front of the desktop in a small side room. I was entering the new intake information of surrendered and found pets on our online adoption page. For each dog that was ready to be offered for adoption, I'd enter the animal's ID number, gender, breed, age, size and location in the kennel. A photo was posted alongside the description. It was basically the same task for cats. True to form, there were a couple new cats today and several dogs.

I had just finished the lot when an employee walked past the office door with a large dog on a leash. The dog didn't look like any that I had posted that morning on the organization's website. I jumped up to have a look.

"Carrie!" I called out. "Hold on!" She stopped in the hall and waited for me to catch up. "Is this a new incoming?"

Carrie placed a professionally manicured hand on the head of the large multi-colored dog. "Yeah, she was found in the Tenth Ward yesterday. Tied to a signpost." She shook her head in disgust. "The person who noticed her tried to find the owner by knocking on doors and posting on Facebook, but no one claimed her. She wasn't even listed as missing. Can you believe it?"

No, I couldn't. This was a beautiful dog. I knew enough about canine coat colors to recognize her as a blue merle, and enough about AKC dog breeds to identify her as a smooth-coated collie. She had a white chest and full white collar with patches of fur that were browns and muted bluish-gray tones. I drew closer and held out my hand (not professionally manicured) which she sniffed gently, with much concentration. A tender lick followed. I was in love.

I knelt, and placing my hands on either side of the dog's narrow head, massaged her silky face and ears. As my eyes met the collie's alert bright blue ones, I asked Carrie if the paperwork had been submitted yet.

"Yes," Carrie answered, "the front desk has it. Abbey, you know we have to keep her for five days to see if anyone claims her before we can put her up for adoption." She sighed. "No ID tag, but we did find a spay scar. You can list her on the Recently Found page."

"Oh, I know," I said. "I… I'm…"

Carrie laughed at my stammering, threw her head back, her blond undercut pixie splaying in all directions.. "You are a sketch, you are! You love this dog already. Don't set your heart on her, though, because you're sure to have it broken when the owner comes in to claim her."

Carrie continued down the hall with the collie. I stood. "What name should I give her on the website?"

Carrie glanced back at me. "You have five days to think about it. No name unless she's not claimed."

I called out, "Is she microchipped?"

"We'll find out. The scanner is charging!" She and the lovely collie turned the corner.

"Do you need help washing her?" I asked the empty hallway. Sagging in defeat, I returned to my desk. Someone had placed the collie's intake form in front of the computer for me while I was talking to Carrie. I opened another window and began typing on the page showing animals newly brought in. ID #: 82526. Gender: Female. Breed: shorthair mix. *That's not correct, but I'll let it go.* Age: approx.. 2 years. Size: 40 lbs. I also noted the date surrendered with information about how to claim her for the owner. I uploaded the stunning dog's photo with reluctance. On this page of the website, I usually inserted a title, like "Are You Missing Me?" or "Do You know Me?" Today I didn't, and I didn't question my intentions.

I looked at the time and realized that I had to leave in order to make it to the Agathas lunch meeting. I shut down the computer, grabbed my purse and sweater and hurried down the hall. Raising my hand in a wave, I called out to my co-workers. "Bye, all, see you next week!" A chorus of responses followed me as I cruised through the double doors.

When I reached the church parking lot, I took my belongings, including the turkey sandwich I had made at home that morning, to the Memorial Parlor on the building's main floor. It was twelve noon on the dot, and I could hear a hodgepodge of conversation coming from inside the room. Around the wooden banquet table sat five members of the Agathas. I felt a bit out of breath as I approached the women and the empty seat that was, I hoped, reserved for me. All chattering stopped, and I had five pairs of eyes on me.

"Greetings, all." I said, and hurried to the table. "I'm not late, am I?" I sat down between Nina and Lillian and placed my sandwich bag in front of me. I flashed a brief smile and a collection of voices welcomed me to the group. Feeling like a student late for an exam, I frantically tried to find something "grown up" to say.

Marjorie hopped up and inquired, "Coffee, tea, water?"

"Coffee's fine," I answered and looked around the table. I had chosen wisely, as everyone else had a coffee cup at their place.

Marjorie filled my cup from a silver percolator with what appeared to be very strong brew, and I couldn't help being reminded of my brother Vince's penchant for coffee that would put hair on your chest. He swore by his ancient percolator he'd inherited from our mother.

"You know everyone, don't you, Abbey?" Marjorie inquired.

"Oh, sure." I smiled again at everyone seated at the table. I recognized Helen Emery, Nina McGarrity, Ruthie Partridge, and Lillian Baird. "Good to see you all."

Lillian spoke up. "Let's bless the food before we dive in, shall we?" We all bowed our heads as Lillian murmured a brief prayer. Instead of closing my eyes, I took that moment to appraise the table top. Everyone had a sandwich on a paper plate, a napkin and utensils in addition to a coffee cup. The abundance of food surprised me. There were chips, pickles, crackers, a tomato and cucumber salad, and a fruit salad.

"Amen!"

I lifted my head with a jolt. Maybe I was a tad late with my own Amen, but no one seemed to notice. Reaching for the cut glass creamer in front of me, I asked, "So, how long has the group been meeting? You started before I was hired, I know that."

"I joined about ten years ago, and the group started a few years before that," Ruthie said. She looked at her friends. "Marjorie and Helen, I think you've been in the group the longest, haven't you?"

Helen sipped her tea. "Yes, Marjorie and I have been attending the longest, then Ruthie, then Nina, and then Lillian. Isn't that right?" The four other ladies nodded in agreement.

Nina sighed with a heavy heart and glanced at her friends. "I miss Carol Ann."

Helen patted her hand in a comforting manner and said. "We all do, dear." Helen looked over at me and explained, "Carol Ann passed away last month from cancer."

I nodded and replied, "I'm so sorry."

Conversation turned to what had been happening in the daily lives of the friends since they had last met.

The summer months had been busy ones for all. Lillian and Marjorie had spent lots of time with their families, especially grandchildren. I imagined the whole hour could have been monopolized with tales of cute kids if Lillian hadn't broken the spell.

"Abbey, you must tell us about the incident you had with the stolen Hopper watercolor." Lillian declared. "All we know is what was in the news. Give us your first-hand account!"

"Yes! Please do!" echoed Helen.

Without notice, I was suddenly in the spotlight.

I had to laugh. You would have thought I was a celebrity.

"Well, let me begin by saying always be aware of your surroundings when you're out and about. Thankfully, I was, and that's how I first figured out I was being followed." The women concurred with my advice and reacted by focusing on my narrative and murmuring agreement. I spent the next few minutes regaling my new friends with the story of the discovered art.

"Weren't you scared for your safety?" Marjorie asked.

"Of course," I said, "especially before I had the security system installed." I shuddered at the memory. "I sometimes felt as if I was being watched." My comment had the women wide-eyed, so I hurried to lessen their fears. "But it all turned out well in the end."

Huge sighs all around. I decided to move the conversation on to the reason for the meetings. "So, tell me why you gather every week, besides lunch, that is. What types of problems do you try to solve?"

Ruthie leaned in front of Lillian and said to me, "We have a really good track record, if I must say so myself." *Track record?* I leaned in to hear more.

Nina offered, "I really can't remember when we've been at a loss for solving any." She cast her eyes around the table, and the other women bobbed their heads in agreement.

I relaxed in my chair, leaning back. "So, what have you worked out lately, before you disbanded for the summer?"

"Let's see," Marjorie began. "Our last meeting of the year is different from others in which we address problems that often affect us personally. The final lunch is always a brain teaser. Just to set us off with a puzzle we know we can solve. Last June was the one about matching names with their professions."

I tilted my head and frowned, confused.

Marjorie explained, "Are you familiar with word problems?"

I understood then. "I am. Can you explain to me the one you solved?"

"I will!" Ruthie spoke up. "There are four men named Allan, Bob, Charles and Donald. Their professions, not in name order, are teacher, lawyer, doctor and mechanic. Four statements are made." She began counting on her fingers. "One, Allan and the teacher are on bad terms with Charles. Two, Bob is friends with the doctor. Three, Charles is related to the doctor. And four, the teacher is a friend of Donald and the mechanic. The object is to pair up each name with his profession."

Ruthie's statement was met with silence. "What?" she asked. "I can't help it if my brain works differently from everyone else's."

I was stunned. *How on earth was she able to recall all that?*

Lillian smiled at me as if I were her grandchild. "Ruthie's been working on her eidetic memory."

Helen added, "It's sort of like a photographic memory."

Recovering from my surprise, I asked, "And what is the answer?"

Marjorie said, "Allan is the doctor."

Ruthie stated, "Bob is the teacher."

From Lillian, "Charles is the mechanic."

And Nina offered, "Donald is the lawyer."

I sat there, shaking my head in amazement, when Helen stood, smiling, and declared, "Time for dessert!"

Chapter 3

As Helen marched over to the kitchenette to get the next course, the rest of us cleared the table to make room for the scrumptious end to the meal. When she reappeared with the tiered glass plate, it definitely had been worth the wait.

She placed the four-inch high coconut layer cake on the table in front of her place, and amid the comments of admiration proceeded to slice pieces for all of us and hand them around. Marjorie, meanwhile, refilled the coffee cups like a woman on a mission.

The ladies tucked into the cake as if they were ravenous. Holding back laughter, I listened to all the culinary moans of bliss emanating from the mouths of the ladies surrounding me. It sounded like the final scene of a cooking show when the chefs are tasting what they had created.

I took a small forkful. "This is absolutely divine, Helen," I complimented her. "Are the desserts always this good?"

My question elicited a sudden calm to the table.

"Mm, n-no," Nina said with a slight hesitation. "Sometimes we act as guinea pigs for new recipes that aren't always…" She hesitated.

"Tried and true, shall we say?" Lillian suggested. There was a rush of agreement from the others.

I said, "I'm going to take a guess and say that this cake is not an experiment, though, right? It really is too perfect." I ate another piece, with more gusto this time.

Helen gave her head a little bow in my direction, her long gray hair swinging forward. "Touché, Abbey. We did want to impress."

I grinned broadly. "And that you have!" I raised my coffee cup. "To Helen and the white coconut cake!"

The women joined me. "Here, here!"

After replacing my cup in its saucer, I said, "Marjorie lured me here with the fact that you solve problems at your meetings. Is there one you plan to work on today?"

"Actually, I have a concern," Nina rearranged her purple and yellow silk neck scarf. "If no one else minds?"

"Go ahead, Nina," Marjorie urged.

She sat up straighter in her chair, seeming to bolster courage, and began. "A fellow from my bridge club at the community center, Arthur Blish, passed away a couple weeks ago. He was quite well-to-do and had very few family members to whom he would leave his estate. He had two older sisters. Mary and Helene, and one nephew Tony, who is the only son of his late brother and his wife."

"So, three beneficiaries, right?" Ruthie asked. "Mary, Helene and Tony."

Nina nodded. "That's right. My neighbor happens to be one of the sisters. She told me that Arthur left the bulk of his estate to her and her sister, and only a couple thousand dollars to Tony." When Nina paused, I could feel the atmosphere change in the room. All the friends sat up straight, eyes on Nina. All coffee cups clinked in their saucers, and it appeared that each woman was about to speak.

Nina held up her hand, palm forward to thwart off an onslaught of comments. "Here's the dilemma. It seems that Tony has found a second will, and it is dated later than the one the lawyer has."

"Oh, I knew it!" Ruthie cried out, pounding her fist on the table. The cups and saucers all jumped in unison, and even I was startled in my seat. "It has to be a con!"

"A hustle," Helen added.

"Yes, he's trying to swindle his aunts!" Marjorie added, half rising from her chair.

"Wait," Lillian cautioned. "We don't know if the terms of the will were changed in Tony's favor or not." She gazed across the table. "Nina?"

"Yes, they were. Now, Tony has been bequeathed the millions and each aunt only a few thousand."

This news brought a stillness to the room. The huge mahogany mantle clock on the fireplace ticked off the seconds while each woman pondered intensely.

"Do you know this Tony at all, Nina?" asked Helen. "I mean, is he the sort to attempt to take advantage of his relatives?"

"No, I don't, but of course, Mary, my friend does. And she and her sister are none too impressed with Tony's character. He's about forty and hasn't been able to hold a steady job for years. After high school he never really applied himself to learn a trade." She took a taste of her coffee. "College wasn't an option for him."

"Why not?" Ruthie asked with a frown. "No money?"

"I think if he had wanted to go to college, his uncle would have helped him," Nina said. "Mary told me that Arthur was beyond generous. But since Tony did practically nothing to help himself, Arthur withdrew any significant support in the end."

Marjorie suggested, "He probably wasn't someone who wanted to continue sitting in a classroom for the next four years after graduation." The women sat silently with various looks of concern on their faces, as if considering how Tony could have been given a different start to adulthood.

"Where did he find the will?" Lillian asked.

"In a huge old CIA cookbook in Arthur's library," Nina said. "Between pages 121 and 122, he told Tim, the lawyer."

"The CIA put out a cookbook?" Helen pondered aloud. She scoffed. "That in itself sounds odd. What kinds of recipes are they, I wonder. 'How to bake secret messages in a loaf of bread'? Or, 'upside down cake using northern spy apples'?" Her joke triggered a few giggles.

"And what young man uses a cookbook these days, anyway?" Ruthie said to more laughter.

Nina said, "Not *that* CIA. The Culinary Institute of America."

While they had been having their jollies, my brain had wandered in a different direction.

"He seemed pretty sure that's where he found it?" I asked.

"Oh, yes," Nina said. "He's been very sure about all the facts surrounding his discovery of it. He never deviated from his story."

"And I'm pretty certain that's just what it is. A story." I had everyone's attention then.

"What? How do you know?" Their questions shot at me like invisible projectiles. Rising from the table I strolled to the wall of books that served as the church's library. Running my index finger along the spines,

I plucked a well-worn copy of *Tea Time with the Lord*, a book of devotions, and handed it to Nina.

"Find pages 121 and 122," I told her.

Nina dutifully flipped through the book to page 121.

I handed her my paper napkin. "Now, place this napkin between pages 121 and 122."

Nina's eyes sparkled as she shot me a wide grin. "It's impossible!" She held up the book for the others to see. "122 is on the back of 121!"

The room erupted in shouts and applause. I performed a brief bow and returned to my seat. After sipping my coffee, I asked demurely, "May I come back next week?"

Chapter 4

I was at home in front of the television, enjoying a bowl of pistachio pineapple frozen custard after my Chinese takeout, and watching a rerun of a show on television. My late afternoon workout at the neighborhood martial arts dojo having been quite a tough session, I felt a dish of frozen custard was warranted. The scrumptious coconut cake from the Agathas meeting was a distant memory by the time I was finished exercising. After scraping as much as I could from the bowl with my spoon, I set it on the coffee table. *If I had a dog, I'd give her the bowl to lick clean.* The thought stopped me in my tracks. *Whoa, where did that come from?* But of course, I knew.

I muted the TV and opened my laptop to the city animal services website. Not to admire my own handiwork, but to read over the information about the beautiful collie again. Oh, this was not good for me, a person ambivalent about dog ownership. I wanted to talk with someone who could counsel me, but anyone I'd call had either a dog or cat and would surely urge me to get the dog. But then I thought about Carrie's words, that I shouldn't get attached because her owner would claim her soon. *But the dog was abandoned. No one's going to step up and be concerned about her welfare. Oh, well, in for a penny, in for a pound.*

I studied the collie and began thinking about names. It would have to be a name befitting the gorgeous girl that she is. And her background as a herding dog. But she probably hadn't done any herding. Most people don't think about that activity unless they live on a farm or ranch. Well, if I got her, I'd look into that. I shut down my computer and headed off to bed. The lovely collie filled my dreams, wanting to know what I would be naming her.

The next day after I finished my morning walk, I showered and caught the *Kiera* bus to the church. Each of Rochester's buses was decorated on a rear panel with the name of a driver's child or grandchild in lovely script. I made it a goal to recognize as many different ones as I could. Just another quirky city fact I loved. But first, my bakery stop.

Behind the counter of the Brooks Bakery, Jane was busy as could be stocking a cookie tray, and I patiently waited for her to finish and give me her attention. Her ever-present calm was surely a godsend during the bakery's morning rush. For once, I happened to walk in during a lull in the action.

"Abbey! What can I get you?"

"Morning, Jane," I replied. "How about a croissant and one of those chocolate earthquake cookies? And a blueberry muffin, please."

"You got it." She pulled out a piece of tissue paper and reached for the pastry. "Busy day today?"

"Just the usual Friday, but you know that sweet tooth of mine. So can I have a lemon bar, too?"

Jane looked at me with smiling eyes. "Are you planning to do some extra workouts this weekend?"

Placing a ten dollar bill on the counter, I leaned forward and whispered, "I'm thinking of adopting a dog."

"Omigosh! That's great!" Her eyes widened. "From downtown?"

I sighed. "Yes, from the shelter, but it has nothing to do with Sean. We're just friends." Jane knew about my acquaintance with the director after our chance meeting here in the store. I took my bag and Jane took the bill. "Put the change in the jar."

"Thanks, muchly!" Jane looked to her left and stretched her shoulders. "Good, no one behind you." I took that as an opportunity to chat.

"So, there's this women's group at the church that meets once a week. They call themselves the Agathas, and they solve problems at their lunches. I was invited, so I went yesterday."

Jane looked down, straightening her apron. "Really? What's it like?"

"Well, yesterday I helped them solve the case of an heir who forged a will. They work on all kinds of things, I think." I tipped my head, studying her face. "Why? Do you have a concern?"

She studied the bulletin board on the wall behind me. "Me? Um…" She licked her lips before saying, "Not me, really, but my aunt. She thinks there might be a problem with her neighbor." Her eyes darted around the small shop and then met mine. She leaned close. "She thinks there might be a dogfighting ring in that house."

This time, *my* eyes widened in surprise. "Really? But doesn't your aunt live near the university?"

Jane shrugged. "Living in a predominately white-collar neighborhood doesn't mean strange things don't go on. Criminal things, even."

"True. I'll tell you what, Jane. I'll call one of the Agathas and let her know about your dilemma. I'm sure they'll want to speak with you. Do you think you could meet with us on your lunch break next Thursday? Say, noon to one o'clock?"

Jane clasped her hands in relief. "Oh, yes! Let me know what they say. I can be there for the full hour if I know ahead of time. I'm sure someone will cover me for an extra half hour."

The bell on the door jingled then with the next customer and I knew I had to be on my way. "I'll let you know on Monday, okay?"

Jane beamed and gave me a thumbs up as I left the bakery.

Once in the church office, I settled into the Friday routine of printing the Sunday bulletin. When I had finished in the early afternoon, I looked up Marjorie Briscoe's phone number in the directory. She answered promptly with a cheery "Hello!"

"Hi, Marjorie, it's Abbey Quill. Do you have a minute?"

"Certainly, Abbey, what can I do for you?"

"Well, the aunt of a friend of mine is worried about a possible dogfighting ring in her neighborhood." Marjorie gasped in my ear. "Would it be all right if Jane joined us next Thursday? The group might be able to help her. Give her suggestions on how her aunt can approach it."

"That is serious," Marjorie said. "Of course she can come. We can listen to her problem on Thursday and think about the best way to move forward. Dog fighting! Awful."

"Thanks, Marjorie, I appreciate it. See you next week." I left the office, feeling that next Thursday would be a remarkable day.

Chapter 5

The afternoon felt right for pizza-for-one, so I got off the bus at the Pizza Fave on my way home. I jaywalked across Lake Avenue to the store. Other than the bakery, this was my favorite sensory-assaulting venue. When I pushed open the door, Jim was sliding a large pie into the huge oven. The blast of heat along with the aroma of earlier baked crust hit me and I almost stopped in my tracks. He turned and saw me.

"Abbey!" Jim walked over with a smile. "How are ya? One slice or two?"

"Well, I was thinking two, but maybe a small pie to get me through the weekend. How about one with pepperoni, artichokes and ricotta?"

"Sounds good. Fifteen minutes."

Jim's son was at the register, so I paid ahead of time and left a tip in the jar. I found an empty table near the counter and sat down in the plastic chair to wait. The restaurant had been a favorite of mine for years. It was standing room only at lunch time during the week, the line stretching out the door and down the street past the neighboring storefront. I knew that later on tonight the place would be buzzing as people stopped on their way home. In the winter season it was a popular destination for pizza, calzones and rolls before the hockey games.

While I waited, I checked emails and social media on my phone. Smiling, I caught up with the antics of the playful otters. *So cute.*

"Abbey!"

That was a fast fifteen minutes. I jumped up and took the hot cardboard container in both hands. "Thanks, Jim. Have a good weekend."

"You, too, and don't tilt that!" He said, and he turned back to prepare someone else's order. I balanced the pizza box with my hip and pulled the door open. Stepping out onto the sidewalk, I noticed that the traffic had picked up, so I walked to the corner and waited at the light to cross over to the bus stop.

I had just enough time to get the pass out of my pocket when a new hybrid bus rumbled to a stop. Joining the line of passengers, I found a couple of empty seats near the back door and placed the pizza next to me by the window. As I held it in place with one hand, I gazed at the panorama passing by. At a traffic light, I focused on a young man walking two huge dogs. They pulled on the leashes, towing the owner along behind as he dug in his heels for balance. I almost laughed because he reminded me of when I forgot to release the emergency brake on the Beast and the car would skip along the street. But then I recalled Jane's concern about dog fighting and the grin left my face.

None of the three looked as if they were enjoying their walk. Nor did they look at all friendly, and I sensed I wasn't the only one who had that thought. Other pedestrians veered out of the path of the trio who marched along as if they owned the sidewalk. When the light turned green, they all were left behind as the bus continued on its way north toward my home.

On this late afternoon in October, I enjoyed a beer and pizza out on my deck. Rochester was a popular town for the local tv meteorologists. The saying about waiting five minutes for the weather to change was true. That's what made the forecasts like spins on a roulette wheel. After the sultry day, I watched the clouds gather over the lake and slipped my cotton sweater around my shoulders. The temperature must have dropped ten degrees while I sat there eating, and the gusty breeze made it feel cooler.

Saturdays, I usually made it a point to do a workout at the dojo, but for tomorrow I decided to go power walking and skip the martial arts. I wanted to go back to the animal shelter. With that in mind, I called my brother in Wyoming.

"Abbey! What's up?" Vince was one of those perpetually happy people, especially when he was busy. And these days he was busy building and promoting his hemp farm.

"Oh, just checking in. How are things in the marijuana trade?" I leaned back and stretched my legs out.

"Hemp, Abbey, HEMP. And it could not be better. Hold on." I heard him shout to his huge dog, Diesel. "GET OUT OF THERE!" Diesel must have obeyed, because Vince was right back on the line. "He's a great fella, but he can't seem to keep his nose out of the compost pile. I just turned it over yesterday. So, to what do I owe the pleasure?"

I took a deep breath. "I'm thinking of getting a dog."

"Well, well, well. Gonna listen to the old brother, huh?" I could hear a hint of satisfaction. "Talk to me."

"You were right," I admitted. "I do feel the desire for another living, breathing individual in my house." I quickly added, "And there's nobody set to move in on the horizon." I chose not to tell him that I sometimes forgot to set the house alarm. "I could use the security of a dog like Diesel, I think."

"Omigod, you do not want a monster like Diesel!"

"Oh, I agree. I saw a dog at the shelter yesterday, and if her owner doesn't claim her within five days, I want her."

"Okay," Vince said. "Tell me about her."

"She's a blue-eyed merle collie," I began.

"What? Like Strider?" He was referring to rock and roll singer's beloved collie from the 1970's.

"Yes, only she's a smooth collie, not a rough coated. Oh, Vince, the way she looked into my eyes..." I released a huge sigh. "She practically begged me to take her home." I took a swig of my cream ale.

"You're not drinking are you? Too much of that will distort your judgment."

I laughed out loud. "So says the expert!"

"Well, from a security standpoint, collies are hugely protective of their owners. Add to that they're smart and have a great personality—

"We're talking about a dog, not a date, Vince."

"I'm serious, Abbey. She'd be a great catch. And you'd have a companion on your walks, too."

"Yeah, there's that." I thought about how vulnerable I had been feeling since the break-in at my house. "Most all my friends and neighbors have a dog or cat. I don't think a cat would help me feel safe like a dog would."

I heard a phone ring in the background on Vince's end. "Gotta go, Sis. That's work. Sometime over the weekend I'll send you a list of stuff you should get for your new boarder. Loveyoubye."

"Thanks, love you, too," I said to dead air.

After cleaning up, I spent more time on my computer, reading the national canine organization's traits and characteristics of the collie. The more I read, the more I was determined to rescue the blue-eyed merle.

Saturday morning after my walk, I drove to the shelter to spend some time with the collie. Since it was a weekend, the place was pretty busy, and I had to squeeze past several people in the lobby. I saw Mark Sullivan, the admin, at the front desk and, thankfully, he was not assisting anyone.

"Morning, Mark!" I greeted him.

"Hey, Abbey! What brings you—oh, wait, it's that collie, right?"

"Yeesss," I dragged out the word into three syllables. *Does everybody know I've fallen for the collie?*

"Let me check on her." He typed, looking at his computer. "She's still here. But it's only been two days. If unclaimed, she will be available next Tuesday." He sat back and said, "She could probably use some exercise."

I recognized the canine code word for "walk." I took a step forward and my hand shot up in the air. "I volunteer!"

Mark snorted and said, "You *are* a volunteer, Abbey."

I laughed at myself. "Come on, Mark, just take me to her, please."

We walked down the hall toward the kennels and I grabbed a couple poop bags from one of the wall-mounted containers. "Can't have too many of these, right?" I hurried to catch up with him. "So, you recognized her as a smooth collie, too?"

Mark led me around the corner to the left and then the first right. "Oh, sure. My grandparents had one for a long time; I think he lived to be about thirteen. He was a sable, though. Named him Maverick. From the movie, you know? Smart. Fast." The fourth enclosure on the left was our destination. He took his key ring from his pocket and unlocked the door to the wire enclosure while I reached for the leash hanging alongside.

As he twisted the latch and slid open the door, the collie stood, her tail waving slowly, left, right, left, right. Mark stepped aside so I could enter and said, "You know the routine. She's had breakfast already, so there's really no rush to get her back in here." He left the door open as I placed the slip lead around the dog's neck. Walking away, he remarked, "Have fun, and don't take her home, Abbey!"

"No promises," I whispered. And the two of us made our way out to the building's fenced-in play yard.

Chapter 6

I spent about an hour Saturday morning with the collie. She was truly an amazing dog and I loved discovering what commands she knew. She had obviously had some beginning obedience training because she easily understood sit, stay and down. I decided to test her on a couple other advanced directions that I had found online.

After placing her in a sit position, I removed the leash, walked a few feet away and called her to me. "Come!" She ran up and attempted to jump up on me. Yikes! I backed away and quickly said "Off!" and she immediately sat. *Well, well, aren't you a smart one?* She was able to remain in the sit position for a couple minutes while I stood several feet away. *Impressive.* But enough of that. We had to play.

By the back door was a basket of toys, and I had put a tennis ball from it in my pocket on our way out. I gave it a good pitch across the yard. "Go get it!" The collie looked up at me as if to say, "Really?" but she gamely trotted over and picked up the ball. She stood there. "Come!" I called, and waved her over. She returned, taking her time like a human child having to leave the playground, and laid the ball at my feet. She then proceeded to find a far corner of the yard in which to do her business.

Watching her sniff around the grass for "P-mail" from other dogs, I began making my way back to the building and saw that Carrie had come out to watch. She chose a white plastic chair to sit in while studying us.

"Smarter than the average bear, isn't she?" Carrie said, when I reached her.

"You got that right." I felt a distinct nudge on my leg. There the collie was, having caught up to me. I reached down with both hands to scratch behind her ears.

"Only three more days," Carrie remarked. "I'm really hoping you get her. I know she should go home to her owner, but every hour the chance becomes slimmer that she'll be claimed. Oh, we didn't find a microchip." She rose from the chair.

"It's not always the best policy for the owner to get a dog back," I said thoughtfully. "Even though she doesn't appear abused, we have no idea what her home situation was like." I rationalized further. "Maybe the owners moved and couldn't take her with them. Maybe there's a new baby in the home and they didn't feel up to dealing with the dog, too."

Carrie gave me a quick thumbs up and then held the door, and the three of us headed back in to the kennels. Three more days. I ran my hands through my hair and let out a heavy sigh.. *Three days?* I thought. *Hang in there, Abbey.*

True to his word, on Sunday morning Vince sent me a list of supplies I needed to think about. He noted that I could get the basic necessities and keep the receipts in case the owner claimed the dog and I had to return them. That made sense, but in my heart I knew she was mine. I spent the afternoon looking up the items on a popular pet supply site online, and I printed out a list.

That afternoon, I headed to the local pet emporium and cruised the aisles. Absolutely mind boggling. I filled the shopping cart with food, dishes, dental chews, a leash and collar. Considering the collie's disinterest in playing fetch with the tennis ball, I decided on a cloth dragon toy with a squeaker inside. I had read that dogs loved them, and we could play tug of war with it.

I also decided on a bed. Like everything else for pets, the offering was astounding. Finally choosing a large round one made of memory foam over another with a common foam-filled cushion, I placed it on top of everything else in the cart, the mountain now taller that I was.. Pushing it blindly toward the front of the store, I wished it had had a bell or horn on it. I bleated out, "Excuse me! Sorry!" every few feet. At the checkout, a cashier with bright red curls peeked at me from around the pile.

"You can leave the bed in the cart, and just put the smaller things on the belt," she said.

"Okay, thanks." I enthusiastically began placing stuff on the conveyor.

The cashier smiled at me as she began scanning. "First dog?"

I stopped in mid grab of a food bowl. "That obvious, huh?"

"You work here long enough and it's easy to tell." She filled two bags and squeezed them into the cart around the bed while I got out my credit card. "That'll be $259.20."

"What?!" My mouth dropped and my hand clenched my card just as I was about to insert it into the card reader. I leaned closer, across the conveyor belt to examine the register. "I think you need to check the prices. That's an awful lot." I smiled at her, full of hope. I didn't dare admit to not checking the prices of anything.

She laughed out loud and said, "No, ma'am, this is the cost of pet ownership these days. Is there something you want to remove?" When I shook my head, she encouraged me, "Just tap or insert your card."

I know I must have held the expression of disbelief as we waited for the two-foot-long receipt to print. She ripped it off with flourish and said, "Thank you, and come back again!" She added in a stage whisper, "It gets easier, don't worry."

Walking like a zombie to my car, hand clenching the receipt and barely seeing where I was going, I just missed ramming the cart into my vehicle. I gently arranged my purchases in the trunk, since they definitely were precious cargo at that price, and returned the cart to the nearest corral. Back in the car I added up the numbers on the receipt using my phone's calculator app. *Nope, no mistake.* I sighed and slouched in my seat. *But she's worth every penny,* my inner voice spoke to me. A smile of satisfaction erased the furrow of my brow and cheered me enough to sit up, and I turned the key in the ignition.

When I pulled into the driveway, my next door neighbors Natalie and Joyce were busy sprucing up their yard. Seymour, their huge dog, was stretched out on the front porch until he heard my car. I used my remote to open the garage door and pulled the car inside. Seymour greeted me as I unlocked the trunk.

"Hey there, buddy," I said. "Guess what's in Abbey's car!" I pulled out the dog bed first after the lid popped open. Out of the corner of my eye I watched as Joyce and Natalie strolled over.

"What's that?" Natalie eyed me suspiciously. "Seymour doesn't need a new bed."

"It's not for Seymour," I sang.

"No!" Joyce shrieked. "Are you getting a dog?" Seymour began spinning around in circles on the pavement like a canine gyroscope. "That's a huge bed! What on earth are you getting?"

"Grab those two bags for me? This way." I led the three into the kitchen. Natalie and Joyce placed the bags of dog necessities on my table as I propped up the bed against a wall. "Have a seat. I have beer!"

Chapter 7

As my neighbors seated themselves at the table, I set down three cream ales and poured a bag of kettle chips into a bowl. A glance at the wall clock showed four o'clock. "This may ruin your dinner," I commented.

Natalie contemplated, then said, "I don't think so." She took a handful of chips.

"Nope." Joyce. "Don't worry about dinner. We need the dog story." We clinked bottles. Seymour settled on the floor, gazing out the window and checking for squirrels.

I made myself comfortable at the table and my friends leaned in. "So," I took a deep breath. "I haven't gotten the dog yet, but I'm hoping her owner doesn't claim her."

"Oh, so from the shelter huh?" Joyce said, "That's great, a rescue!"

"I thought you were against getting a dog," Natalie said. "What changed your mind? The break-in last summer?"

"I'm afraid so, yeah. But, what can I say? I fell in love."

"Tell us all about her," Natalie said. "She must be extraordinary if she changed your mind."

Joyce added, "What breed is she?"

"She's a smooth-coated collie."

Joyce's face lit up. "OMG, a collie!"

"Tell me she has blue eyes!" Natalie practically shouted.

"Affirmative!" I was sort of surprised they were so enthusiastic. We proceeded to have a spirited discussion about collies and the famous people who had owned one.

As I shared with my neighbors the tale of how the collie and I met, I became more comfortable with the realization that I could very soon be sharing my home with the gorgeous dog. But I tried not to get too confident. "I still have to wait until Tuesday. If her owner claims her, I'll be devastated." I began picking at my beer label.

"Do you want to think about names?" said Natalie. "Or is it too soon?"

"Mm, I've tried thinking about some. Any ideas?"

The three of us sat around the table, looking pensive. Natalie tapped her upper lip with her index finger while Joyce sat back with a frown, arms folded. My friends were naturally quite imaginative so I figured they'd be a good source.

Natalie spoke first. "You're not really into video games, are you, Abbey?"

I shook my head. "No, sorry."

"Favorite book characters?"

"How about films, theater?" Joyce said. When I shrugged she asked, "How about musical performers? Does she remind you of anyone?"

"What bands and musicians do you like?" asked Natalie.

"I do like rock bands—"

"Ringo would be a cute name," Natalie suggested.

"—Jazz, R and B, Blues-Rock, Reggae…"

"You like Reggae?" Joyce acted as if I had just said I liked wasabi mustard on a hot dog.

"Marley," I murmured.

Natalie and Joyce's faces lit up at hearing the name. "Yes! Perfect!"

I groaned, covering my face with my hands. "What if I don't get her? What if her owner—"

"Don't think about that right now. Be positive." Natalie reached her hand out across the table to me.

"Yes, be optimistic," Joyce agreed. "We'll maneuver that speedbump if we hit it."

I dropped my hands and took in the smiling, confident faces of the women sitting across from me. "I'm so lucky to have friends like you. Thank you."

"Eh, we're all lucky," Natalie said. She gazed over at Seymour, who had begun snoozing during our conversation, his loose brown lips flapping with every exhale. "And the bruiser will have a friend, too."

"I'm glad he can't hear us," Joyce said, "in case it doesn't happen."

"It *will* happen, Abbey," Natalie determined, and gave her partner a sideways glance. "Don't listen to Debby Downer here."

"Thanks for your support. You know I'll be hounding you with questions a lot." I smiled. "No pun intended."

My friends groaned, and Joyce said, "We need to get going. We're meeting friends for dinner at that new Italian place on Lake Avenue." She and Natalie rose from the table. "Come on, Seymour."

We walked out to the back deck. "Have a good time, and be sure to let me know how it is, " I called after them. "Especially the Fettuccini Alfredo!" The trio crossed the back yard to their home and disappeared through the hedge gate with a wave from Natalie.

After turning on the oven, I popped in a couple slices of pizza. By the time I had finished making a salad, the slices were warm and I sat down to eat. With my laptop open in front of me, I dined while surfing the internet. Thinking back to my conversation with Jane on Friday about her aunt's concern, I found my way to the topic of dog fighting. Not the best subject to peruse while eating.

The first article to pop up on the screen was not one about an organized fight, but it detailed the attack of a smaller dog by two others while on a walk with its owner at the local beach. The dog died at the scene, and I felt a visceral tug on my gut when I read about it. *Oh, poor baby.* There was a photo of the pup, pre attack. My eyes welled up and I left that site with a speedy tap to the keyboard.

Scrolling on, I noticed one about a pit bull that was credited with cracking a local dogfighting ring by working undercover. Now that was an interesting article.

An investigator went undercover several years ago, asking around for a place to fight his dog. It wasn't more than a couple days when the investigator was contacted by a major member of the ring. With all communications recorded by the investigator, Atlas didn't have to fight, and he was retired with honors to accompany his handler on publicity visits. I sat back in my chair. *Wow!* I thought about how easily that could have gone south.

Okay, I had had enough. I turned off my computer and headed upstairs to bed to listen to a comedy podcast so my dreams wouldn't be compromised by bad vibes.

Chapter 8

At the bakery the next morning, I told Jane that she was welcome to join the Agathas on Thursday. "Noon to one o'clock. Is that okay?" I said.

Jane nodded eagerly. "Perfect! Thanks so much, Abbey." She handed me my white bag holding a croissant and a black 'n' white cookie. "Enjoy your day!"

"You, too," I said, and stuffed a dollar bill into the tip jar. I noted with satisfaction that the line behind me to the door was doubled with customers who didn't want to wait on the sidewalk. I politely squeezed past them on my way out. Jane's store had weathered hard times over the past couple years along with other small businesses. I felt as if my intense sweet tooth and I had played a significant role in that success, and I walked to my car with a jaunty step.

After I had taken a moment for private meditation before starting work, I went about my Monday routine of clearing the sanctuary of discarded bulletins and making sure that all lights and water faucets were turned off from the day before. In the hot weather the Trustees will leave fans on, and in the winter they forget to turn off heaters. I can count on two hands the times the organist left the organ motor running. People will neglect the darndest things in their haste to make Sunday brunch at their favorite eating establishment.

I answered emails and voicemails and noted that there had been no USPS delivery on Saturday. My perusal of the calendar reminded me that the church's anniversary was coming up at the end of the month, marking 120 years in the neighborhood. The church body had been around longer than the current building, having first assembled in the early 1900's. I'm sure this would be a big celebration. They opted to curb expenditures this year and hold the dinner in the church fellowship hall instead of at a local restaurant. Many members of the congregation had either lost their jobs or tightened their belts in other ways to survive during the pandemic. For some, it was difficult just making their pledge commitment. Knowing the church membership as I did, I knew it would be a stellar day no matter where the dinner was held.

I took care of some other office chores, even did a little dusting since the custodian, bless his heart, did the minimum. He was the master of trash removal, but couldn't utilize a vacuum cleaner or dust rag to save his life. Two o'clock rolled around before I knew it, and I was soon driving to the animal shelter to volunteer and see the collie. Fingers crossed she was still there.

Sitting in Mark's seat at the reception desk was someone I hadn't seen before. I approached her and, feeling a tenseness in my stomach, said, "Hi, I'm Abbey Quill, a volunteer. Is the collie still here?" I forced myself to wait for her answer, half turning to jog down the hall to where I knew the dog had last been. Her frown stopped me cold.

"The collie?" she responded. "I'm pretty sure I saw someone take her..."

"What? Really? Oh, no." I deflated.

At that moment Mark stepped into the office. "Thanks, Terry, I'll take it from here." The young woman jumped up as if caught red-handed.

"You're welcome, Mark!" She smiled fondly at him and exited the room, glancing at me over her shoulder with squinting eyes that almost accused me of something nefarious.

I placed both hands on the counter. "Mark, please tell me the collie's owner hasn't been by." I felt the embarrassment of tears forming that I could not control.

"Not gonna play with you, Abbey." He gave me an encouraging smile. "She's still here."

"Oh, thank you." The hollowness disappeared. "I'm just going to say hi and then I'll be back tomorrow to work on the postings. Okay?"

"I understand," Mark waved with a flourish. "Off you go!"

I had to keep myself from sprinting back through the halls to the kennel where *my* collie was. When I came to a halt, she stood there, her tail wagging. We greeted each other through the wires, her nose damp on my fingers.

"I'll be back tomorrow," I told her. "I need to get my exercise in, and then I need to get your new home ready for you." The dog, whom I was already calling Marley in my mind, sat and looked down at her feet. I began to feel apologetic. "Don't worry, Marley, I'll be back bright and early." As if in understanding, Marley stood and again wagged her tail. I placed my hand against the cage and she leaned forward to lick my fingers. With reluctance, I turned and strode toward the front doors.

"See you tomorrow, Mark," I said.

"You will!"

At home I changed into my gi and walked to the dojo where I put in a good hour of exercise. I recognized some of the regulars, but as it was not my usual day to be there, I noticed some new people, too. I was glad to see that the place thrived on days I wasn't there. *Yeah, like I'm so crucial.* As I was leaving the dojo, I held the door for a young woman who had a dog on a leash. I looked at them in surprise.

"Excuse me," I said. "Are dogs allowed in here? I mean, other than service dogs?"

The woman stopped, and so did her shepherd mix. "Sure," she said. "The sensei doesn't mind as long as the dog is well trained and quiet."

"That is so cool." I lowered my hand for the dog to sniff.

"I'm Sharon, and this is Daisy," she said by way of introduction.

"I'm Abbey. I may be getting a dog soon, and I'd love to bring her here while I work out."

"Well, Daisy sits quietly in the corner on her mat that I bring along." Sharon hoisted her duffle. "It should be no problem if your dog behaves."

"Thanks for the info," I said. "And great to meet you both. Better leave you to it."

I watched Sharon and Daisy walked softly down the hall, and I then made my way home.

When I arrived, I showered and changed, and then took all the items I had purchased for Marley out of the bags and arranged them on my kitchen table. Gee whiz, I had bought a lot. Toys, food, bed. *Where will she sleep? Maybe I should have bought two beds. One for downstairs and one for my room?*

At dinner time, my refrigerator revealed very little in the way of fresh food. "Sheesh. I have to go to the store again?" I said aloud. With a sigh I opened the freezer. "Hmm. Breakfast isn't just for breakfast!" I pulled out an opened package of frozen waffles, popped two in the toaster and looked for the maple syrup in the back of the fridge. The jug felt pretty light, so I wrote "maple syrup" on the small whiteboard that displayed my grocery list. With warmed up syrup and butter, I assembled my waffle dinner and a small glass of grapefruit juice on the coffee table for a meal in front of the TV. I sat back in a slouch. Just me and the tube. Again.

Chapter 9

I awoke Tuesday morning with a start. *Marley's Gotcha Day!* After a rushed power walk, shower and coffee, I grabbed the brown leather collar and leash and drove to the shelter. I couldn't remember the last time I had been so excited. Well, there was the time I found the Hopper painting, but that seemed eons ago. Nevertheless, the feeling was the same. Life changing.

I arrived at 8:45 before the building was open and found myself chatting with the police horses that were in the outside pen. Though the conversation was pretty much one sided, it did take my mind off the reason for my impatience. Hearing the shelter's door unlocking across the sidewalk, I hurried away. I don't think the horses minded that I neglected to say goodbye.

Carrie opened the glass panel for me and two employees who had just emerged from their cars. "Good morning, everybody! Come on in." Carrie's smile when our eyes met told me she shared my excitement. "So, today's the big day!"

"Mm hmm. I'm going to exercise her before I start on the postings. Is that okay?" My voice held a slight tremor, and if Carrie noticed my eagerness, she didn't remark on it.

"Sure. She's been out and fed breakfast by now, so a bit of playtime would be nice for her." Carrie looked down at the collar and leash in my hands. "I see you're all ready to take her home." Before I could answer, she continued, "You'll make a great dog mom."

I smiled at the phrase. "Is that the term? Or will I be a 'pawrent?'"

"I've also heard pet parent and dog guardian."

"Hmm, dog guardian. That's a new one," I said.

We stopped at the office and Carrie picked the keys off the board and I left the new leash and collar on a table. Have you decided on a name yet?

"Marley," I replied.

"Oh, beautiful! It's perfect! Let's go say hi to Marley!"

After about ten minutes of play in the yard, I returned Marley to her kennel and sat at the computer desk to work on the online descriptions of incoming animals. There were only a few to post, and I quickly finished and moved on to upcoming events to be placed on social media.

Animal services was hosting an Open House in a couple weeks. People were encouraged to "Come On Down!" and "Find Your Furever Friend!" Adoption fees were being halved and free photos would be taken of any adoptive families. I smiled to myself. Before volunteering at the shelter, I would have discounted this type of event. But now, as a potential "dog guardian," I was happy to see the opportunity for these animals to find loving homes. *My, my, how perspective changes things.*

I then updated the Service's Wish List. The categories remained the same – animal care, clinic, outreach support, transportation, foster care and miscellaneous. But the particular items desired by the shelter often changed weekly. People were really generous with their giving, I learned. Not only did they donate food and supplies, but they donated their time. Witnessing this type of dedication made me smile inside and feel admiration for anonymous strangers who see a need and fill it. It wasn't lost on me that I, too, was not only a volunteer but a recipient of this kindness.

My stomach did a little flip-flop when I saw the time on the computer screen's lower right corner and realized it was almost noon. As I closed down the website, I moved more slowly. *Cold feet, Abbey? No. It's anticipation.* I stepped into the office and questioned Mark hesitantly. " Excuse me, Mark. Who do I see about adopting Ma—the collie? I did fill out an adoption application online."

"Let me make a call," he said, and stopped what he was doing to dial an extension. He spoke briefly with someone on the line. With his mouth tipping up in a knowing smile, he typed something on the keyboard and the printer generated a couple pages. Mark reached over and plucked them from the tray. "Here is your application. Ron will want to go over it with you."

"Thanks, Mark." I turned as soft footsteps sounded behind me.

Mark introduced us. "Abbey Quill, this is Ron Tenney, head of adoptions. Ron, Abbey."

We shook hands. "Good to meet you, Abbey. I've seen you around, but we've always been moving in opposite directions, it seems."

"Same here," I said. "You're a busy guy." We moved away from Mark's desk and stood a few feet away. I handed him my application. As he looked it over, I watched him. He was a couple inches taller than I with dark brown hair, and his short beard had several strands of gray in it. His brown eyes skimmed the pages. I pegged his age at around 40.

"Okay, looks good," he said. "Let's go sit down and discuss what your next steps are."

Next steps? I really hadn't thought much past marching Marley out the door, even though I knew it was more involved than that. I followed Ron down the hall to his office where he sat behind his desk and I took a chair in front.

He smiled at me then. "First, I need to see your identification. Driver's license or any other form of ID."

I fumbled in my wallet for my license and handed it over. With a glance at my photo, he gave it back.

"So, you've never had a dog before. Are you familiar with the type of care and exercise the collie will require?" He took a printed form from a file on the desk.

"Yes," I nodded. "My brother has a huge dog and we've spoken at length about that." I nervously twisted my garnet ring as I commented. "I'm a daily, well, almost daily, walker, and I have neighbors who have a large mixed breed, so…." My voice drifted off.

Ron placed the form in front of me. It was the Adoption Contract. I noticed that the top spaces with my own personal information, and the dog's (microchip number, DOB, etc.), were already filled out. I looked up in surprise.

"If the owner had claimed her, I'd just have shredded this." Ron smiled again. "You come highly recommended."

I had begun reading the contract, so I didn't notice his last comment. The form listed eight items that I had to agree to, from acknowledging receiving the dog to consenting to its care. Finally, it listed the adoption fee of $100 and lines for our signatures.

I looked up when I heard Ron speaking again. "I know you've been interacting with the collie, so you already know her habits and temperament. She's great on the grooming table." *Grooming table?!* "So, either care at home or at a professional groomer's won't be a problem. We've treated her with flea, tick and heartworm medications, so you'll want to continue with that. Our vet made sure she's up to date with her vaccinations." He sat back. "You just need to choose a vet that you'll feel comfortable with."

My mind was reeling since I hadn't thought of a vet. I'd need to ask Joyce and Natalie where they take Seymour.

"Do you have questions for me?" Ron asked. He leaned forward and folded his arms.

"Uh. There was something, let me think. Oh, license? Where do I get that?"

"I suggest going to the city website and click on dog licenses." He tapped the file folder with his index finger. "All the information you need is in here. Proof of rabies vaccination, proof of spay. You'll need to send a check for ten dollars along with copies of the vet records. Renewal is an annual thing."

"Okay. I can't think of anything else at the moment." I reached into my purse for my checkbook and gave Ron payment of the adoption fee. We both signed the contract.

Ron stood. "Let's go get your dog!"

We walked to the office where I picked up the collar and leash and Mark made me a copy of the contract for me. Ron saw Carrie walking toward us down the hall and called out. "Carrie! Want to bring down the collie?"

Carrie did an about face with a fist pump and sped away. It struck me that everyone was really happy for me and Marley. I understood that not all dogs had joyful futures after ending up here.

As Marley and I left the building, I glanced back to see Ron, Mark and Carrie watching and gave them a wave. "See you Thursday!" I said. I held the car's back door open for Marley, and with a huge leap she landed on the back seat. After a couple turns to make herself comfy, she sat facing me, waiting. "Well, then," I laughed. "Let's go home!"

Chapter 10

Instead of heading straight home, I chose to take Marley to the pier for a walk. It was early afternoon and the sky was clear, so I thought we'd enjoy the wide outdoors. I may as well introduce her to one of my favorite places sooner rather than later. The parking lot adjacent to the lake had a scant number of vehicles, but with kids in school and most people working, I wasn't surprised.

With nothing else on my agenda, I let Marley sniff to her heart's content. Several passersby remarked what a pretty dog she was, and so good on lead. My heart filled with pride until I remembered that it was not I who had trained her. Well, thanks to the previous owner, for sure. It still made me feel good.

According to the rules, dogs aren't allowed on the beach boardwalk. But I didn't see any security or police, so what the heck? As we continued our "sniffari" along the walkway, I heard a commotion to my left. Near one of the picnic shelters, a couple people were arguing. As a rule, I try not to be nosy, but they were loud enough to make me stop and listen. The man was grasping the leash of a large, well-muscled, snarling dog, and the woman had a tiny pup in her arms. As she turned to walk away, the large dog lunged and the man lost his grip. The dog was running at the woman, and I couldn't help calling out in warning.

"LOOK OUT! BEHIND YOU!"

The woman turned just in time to confront the raging animal and adjusted her hold on the dog in her arms. I recognized her martial arts move as a round house kick as she swung her leg around, striking the attacking dog under its chin with her foot. The dog performed a flying backward flip in the air and landed with a thud. If it hadn't been such a terrifying situation, I'd have applauded. I wondered where she trained. And what was she wearing, hiking boots?

The owner cradled his now-still dog in his arms as it lay stunned, gasping for breath. Its huge brown chest heaved. The man looked up at the woman, his face full of loathing. His full head of black hair and a matching mustache reminded me of a demon. All he needed was a pair of horns.

"You bitch!" he cried. "You tryin' to kill my dog?"

"Me?" She said incredulously. "Your dog was going to attack me and Puffy!" She stood her ground. "For all I know your monster eats dogs like mine for dinner!" She began backing away, probably realizing that the situation could easily become more volatile.

"Yeah, you better scram, lady," he growled. "Cuz my dog *does* like the taste of puny mutts like yours!"

The woman stumbled a step or two and her face contorted in horror when she realized the guy meant what he said. Her voice shook. "You... you better keep that dog away from us. I'm going to report you."

"Hah." The man looked around, briefly catching me in his sight. "Who to? Your word against mine. Tough luck, lady."

When he turned toward me, I reflexively backed away a step, and I bumped into Marley who had been behind me, shying away from the hostility. I placed a comforting hand on her head.

I watched the woman run off without another word, little Puffy in her arms, and guessed that she knew to get out of a bad situation while she could. I released the huge breath I had unconsciously been holding. While the man continued to examine his dog, Marley and I quickly made our way back down the boardwalk and to my car, and I couldn't help taking a couple glances back at them over my shoulder.

"Sorry for the rude beginning, baby," I said. "We'll meet nicer people another day." Marley just looked at me with her pale blue eyes and appeared to believe every word as she settled on the back seat.

Driving home, I reflected on the scenario at the lake and recalled the article I had read online about the dog attack. I shuddered, thinking that I could have been a witness to a horrible incident. The man's dog looked like a mix that would normally be used for fighting, according to what I had seen online. It also looked like the majority of the dogs that were taken in at the shelter. Pit bull mixes, they were called.

On the shelter's website, I was required to use the term "mixed breed" to describe them, but we all knew they were pit terriers of some sort. I sighed. Some were picked up wandering the streets, others were brought in and surrendered. A number of them, I was told, were simply too docile to engage in fighting. And too many of those poor dogs had literal battle scars.

I glanced in the rearview mirror at Marley, who was now standing on the seat with her nose out the window that I had opened halfway. We were both lucky.

I couldn't wait to introduce her to Joyce and Natalie. My efforts were fruitless, though, as it appeared they weren't home after a good minute of my pounding on their front door and then checking around the back. We went home, leaving Seymour barking at us through the door.

I let Marley become acquainted with her new residence. In typical collie fashion, she walked the perimeter of the back and front yards, taking her time to record every scent and physical detail. Several times she established her ownership by leaving her liquid DNA in strategic spots so other animals would know who the new Queen of the Estate was.

Inside the house, I was momentarily concerned that she might continue that impulse, but no worries. She sniffed at her food bowls, and I filled one with water. Following a drink, she assessed the first floor and found it acceptable. Even better, she decided the bed was just right, and after a couple turns she plopped herself down on it. Marley rested her long nose on her front paws and stared at me.

I stood in front of her with my arms akimbo. "Well, what do we do now, huh, Marley? Oh, wait! Pictures!" After swiping the camera app open on my phone, I took several photos of my new housemate as she lounged. "That's enough glamour shots for now. We can get some action shots later." I placed the phone on the coffee table and sat down on the loveseat. With a leap, Marley was sitting next to me, head on my lap. "You like me, you really like me," I murmured. And we both nodded off for a short nap.

It was 4:30 when my doorbell rang while Marley and I were watching the early edition of the evening news. She jumped up like a shot and ran barking to the door, letting me know that she'd save me from whoever was trying to enter. I opened the door and greeted my neighbors.

"Hi! Come in if you dare!" I laughed. When Marley heard me welcome Joyce and Natalie, she ceased barking and whined a little, and then began her sniffing interrogation, keeping them at the threshold. Both women held out their hands for her to inspect. Satisfied, Marley backed away into the hallway to allow entry.

"I'm glad we passed muster," Natalie said, and Joyce agreed.

I led the couple into the living room, Marley resuming her place next to me on the loveseat. Her head lay on my lap, but she continued to keep a critical eye on the two visitors as they took chairs. My hand stroked her short, thick coat.

Joyce clasped her hands. "Oh, Abbey, she is magnificent. What an amazing blend of colors!" She leaned forward. "I'd love to use her in an ad campaign."

Natalie grinned. "For what? A new product? Wait – "The Merle Look.""

We laughed at that, but Joyce said, "Hey, stranger things have been runaway successes in the makeup industry. Remember the stardust and raccoon looks of the '60's?"

When I looked puzzled, Natalie said, "You don't want to know, Abbey. Some styles are better left buried."

But Joyce continued. "No, really. I can see it already. *The Collie Couture Collection.* With all the collie coat color combinations, it could be really popular!"

Natalie stood. "Come on, hun, let's go. Enough alliteration for one day." To me, she said, "Bring Marley over after dinner to meet Seymour. It'll be a hoot."

Chapter 11

That evening, Marley and I walked through the hedge to Seymour's house. He and his owners were lounging in the yard, enjoying red wine and the orange-violet horizon worthy of a myriad-colored paint display. Seymour jumped up with a start from what to me had appeared to be a deep sleep. His thunderous bark stopped both me and Marley in our tracks.

"Seymour!" Joyce and Natalie shouted simultaneously and rose to meet us where Seymour was refusing us entry. But the dog stood his ground. Seeing his confusion, I imagined him thinking, *Familiar human, but who's this canine?*

I held out my hand to Seymour. He stepped closer to me and to Marley. As he sniffed Marley, his tail began a frenzied wag, and so did hers. Seymour bowed down on his front legs, the universal dog invitation to play. Marley copied him, and they were off on a tear around the backyard.

"No worries there!" Joyce said. Natalie poured me a glass of pinot noir.

I agreed and raised my glass. "Here's to a long friendship!" Following the ritual clinking of glasses, we sat back and watched the two romping dogs for a minute. "I can't help being relieved they get along so well."

"Oh, there was no question," Joyce stated.

"Of course not!" said Natalie. "Seymour's just a big lovey boy."

"Unless you're a burglar," I added. We had a good laugh at that, finding the humor despite the serious event of last summer.

"How old did you say she is?" Natalie asked.

"The vet thinks about two years based on her overall health."

"Well, she sure acts like a puppy, all that energy," added Joyce. "So, what are your plans for her during the days that you're working? Seymour does all right here on his own, but neither of us is gone for more than a few hours during the day."

"Did you buy her a crate?" Natalie asked.

"A... crate? That wasn't on Vince's list." I looked from one friend to the other.

Joyce looked puzzled, too. "Vince's List? What's that, some online pet site?"

Natalie pulled a face and placed her wine glass on the table decisively to make a point. "Really, Joyce? Vince is her *brother.* You have a great memory, but it's short."

Laughing, I reached over as though to relieve Joyce of her wine. "No more for you, dear. Actually, I'm going to take her with me. She can take a break with me, walk around the church property; she's been pretty mellow so far." The dogs were a picture of contentment, resting on the lawn, panting with tongues lolling. "And I met a woman the other day who brings her dog to the dojo while she practices. So long as Marley behaves, no problem."

I suddenly remembered the altercation at the beach. "Speaking of problems, we went for a walk at Ontario this afternoon. It was great until we watched this exchange between two dogs and their owners." Joyce and Natalie listened intently to the details.

When I had finished, they each stated their opinions. Not unexpectedly, we all agreed it was a serious situation and we always had to be alert when out and about with the dogs.

Then, I was reminded of the concern that Jane the bakery owner had about dogfighting in her aunt's neighborhood. I narrated her tale at length. "It's really a problem all over," I said. "I looked up dogfighting online and it's heartbreaking and sickening." We all took a moment and sipped our wine in agreement.

"I think that's what would keep me from working at the animal shelter," Natalie said. "If I had the time, that is." Her voice softened as she added, "It's just too, too much."

Joyce perked up a bit and said, "Well, I sure hope your Agatha group can help Jane and her aunt. It sounds like something they would enjoy getting their teeth into, so to speak." We all groaned at the lame pun.

We sat in a companiable silence for a couple minutes, pleased by the playful dogs who were back at it again. Natalie eventually broke the quiet.

"You know, Abbey, I read that men often find walking their dogs helps them meet women."

My sip of wine turned into a gulp and I almost choked.

"Excuse me?" I gaped at my friend.

"Natalie!" Joyce said, looking appalled.

"What? We talked about this."

"Well, not with *her* we didn't!"

"Oh my God!" I laughed out loud. "You're concerned about my love life?"

Natalie puffed out her ample chest in defense. "We've felt sorry for you since you broke up with that worthless piece of you-know-what a couple years ago. Colin, wasn't it?"

"And remember when you told us about that boy you had a crush on since fifth grade? And you didn't know he liked you until the last day of high school?" Joyce piped up.

"Tommy…" said Natalie, *sotto voce.*

My neighbors were compassionate, and I appreciated that about them. It was touching, their awkwardness and the fact that they were concerned about my social life. I decided to end their misery.

"It's really all right, friends. It's not as if I haven't thought about it myself. I'm not getting any younger, right?" I stood. "And on that note." I called out, "Marley! Here, girl!" Marley came to me on a run, and Seymour wasn't about to be left behind.

"She knows her name already!" Natalie walked around to give Marley a pat and then kissed her long nose. "You come back any time, sweetie!"

"Ditto!" Joyce said. "Have a successful first night!"

I left for home with a wave of thanks, my trusty new buddy at my heels.

We watched an episode of a detective series on one of my streaming services, a fine way to unwind after a significant day. And there was nothing like a good mystery to take my mind off the fact that I did have a non-existent love life. *Good things come to those who wait.* Sometimes, the longer you have to wait for something, the more you appreciate it when you finally get it.

I leashed Marley and we took a short walk down the street. Back at home I gave her a dog cookie and left her downstairs after I locked up the house, and I went up to bed. Of course, she followed. So, I went back down and brought her bed up, placing it on the bedroom floor near the hall.

"There. You can sleep in my room and not be scared on your first night." As if on cue, Marley curled up in a circle on the foam cushion and watched me. Those two unblinking blue eyes were a bit unnerving, so I quickly changed into my pajamas on the other side of the room. Who likes to be stared at when they're taking their clothes off? *Unless... Oh, just stop it! Darn those women, anyway.* I finished up in the bathroom and climbed into bed. After taking another photo of Marley to send to Vince, I placed my phone on the bedside table and turned out the light.

It took all of ten seconds before I felt as if an earthquake had struck my bed. "AAAAH!" My heart leapt in my chest, causing me to sit straight up. I turned on my lamp and there Marley was, curled up next to me. I swear she didn't know that she had almost given me a heart attack. I gulped air and willed my pulse to calm.

"Oh, you are not pulling this, young lady." I am not a fan of allowing dogs to sleep in one's own bed. Nope, no way. I knew how to fix this. I went down to find some tiny dog training treats in the kitchen. Upstairs, I led Marley to her bed, and when she had made herself comfortable, I gave her a couple tidbits. She stayed. I climbed back into bed. Lights out. I heard her get up so I turned on the light. She froze.

"Get back there," I instructed her, pointing to the bed and making eye contact, daring her to defy me. She did as she was told, so I gave her some more treats. We repeated this scenario numerous times until I was able to fall asleep without her in my bed. The last time I looked at my phone it showed 2:00 am.

Chapter 12

Four hours later a wet tongue licked my face. "Yuck!" I burrowed my face deep into my pillow, but I couldn't ignore the creature who was adamant I get up. *Now.*

I threw on clothes, grabbed my keys and dog necessities, and Marley and I performed our morning constitutional. I chose a longer route that took us toward the marina and back home past the dojo. She proved to be a welcome hiking partner, keeping up with me easily, except for the times she pulled me off the sidewalk to smell who knows what. Nearing home, what threw me was the "Sold" sign on the house across the street.

I wrote a mental note to myself to speak with the current owners later in the day and find out where they had finally decided to go. They'd been such good neighbors for so long. I hated that they were moving, but their family had grown too large for the small bungalow. With two children already, they had twins last winter and obviously needed more than two bedrooms.

After a shower and breakfast, I loaded Marley into the car and drove to work. It struck me that I wouldn't be taking the bus anymore, and that saddened me a little, but the gift of Marley helped me feel better about it. What about the times I wouldn't be able or allowed to take her with me someplace? I accepted the idea that I'd have to get a crate if I couldn't trust her alone in the house.

Leaving the dog in the car, I rushed into the bakery and hurriedly gave Jane my order.

"Marley's in the car!" I gushed. "Gotta be quick!"

"Ooh, your dog?!" Jane tossed a croissant and cranberry muffin in the bag and reached for a plain brown cookie shaped like a bone. She added it to the bag.

"Just a welcome treat," she said. "Next time you'll have to pay for it. See you tomorrow!"

"Tomorrow?" I stopped mid-turn.

She laughed and said, "The Agathas Meeting. Remember?"

"Oh, yes! See you at noon!" I exited the shop in which I once preferred to linger and briefly reflected on my shift in priorities. *Me with a dog. Who'd a thunk it?*

Marley was waiting patiently in the car, but she was now in the driver's seat.

"What's this, huh? You don't have a driver's license, sweetie." She moved over as I pushed my way in. "Wait til I show you what Jane gave you!"

At church, she settled down nicely as I went about my routine. We both enjoyed our goodies, and I put some water in a bowl for her that I found in the kitchenette adjacent to the memorial parlor. We took our break at noon, and left for home at two o'clock.

Considering that I needed to shop for groceries, I figured leaving her home for an hour or so would be a good indication on how she handled being in the house alone. Bravely, I closed the kitchen door on her curious face. "I'll be right back. Watch the house!"

I tried not to dawdle, kept looking at my phone for the time, and returned home a little over an hour later. Carrying three large bags, I awkwardly unlocked the door to the kitchen and immediately stepped into a large puddle. *Yikes!*

That hadn't been there when I left. And it spread farther toward the table as I watched it.

"Oh, Marley!"

Marley approached me cautiously, her usually wagging tail still and low. I abandoned the bags on the counter and tore off a wad of paper towels to drop on the puddle. She followed me to the back door where I let her out to the yard. I really felt awful because I should have done that before I left her on her own.

I put away the groceries while casting glances out the window to where she was once again exploring. When she finally approached the door, her "mistake" had been cleaned up and I let her in. She seemed to have recovered her spirit when she understood there would be no scolding from me. Or worse, physical abuse. Maybe her weak bladder had been why she was abandoned. I needed to stop all the speculating. Nothing I could do now but enjoy Marley's company.

I gave her a dog cookie and left her in the kitchen to crunch away. I decided to do some cleaning before dinner and grabbed a dust cloth on my way to the living room. Midway through wiping down the window sill I caught sight of my soon-to-be-ex neighbors arriving home. Well, some of them. I watched as Miriam worked to free the twins from their car seats. I guessed the older kids weren't home from school yet.

"Marley! Here!" I called. She came running, and I hooked her leash and we took off down the driveway.

"Hi, Abbey! Now who is this you brought with you? Don't tell me..." Miriam stood with one twin propped on her hip. I still couldn't tell those babies apart unless they were side by side. To me they looked identical at nine months old, even though they were a boy and a girl. Miriam and James didn't believe in pink and blue.

My face must have been beaming as I introduced Marley. "Yes, I needed company after all."

Miriam reached down with her free hand to greet Marley, who sat politely. "What a beautiful lady. A rescue, right?"

I smiled. "Only the best from the shelter!" I then broached the real reason I had come over. "I saw the 'Sold' sign. Where did you decide to go?"

Miriam looked into the car and saw that twin #2 was still safely ensconced in the land of Nod before speaking. "We found a place that ticked off all the boxes we needed. It's a huge colonial over in the Browncroft neighborhood. Dashiell and Miranda will have to switch schools, but since they're in second grade and kindergarten it won't be too hard an adjustment. Plus, the one they'll attend is in the neighborhood. They can walk instead of taking the bus."

"Wow," I said. "That sounds like a win-win situation."

"Yeah, I think we lucked out."

"So, who did you sell to?"

Miriam shifted twin #1 to her other hip. "A single man. He's a software developer, I think. Maybe video games? I'm not sure. James will remember." She held out the baby to me. "Will you hold Jade a second? I need to get Julian out. His diaper needs changing."

I dropped the leash and found myself with a baby on my own hip, thankful this wasn't the one with the dirty diaper. So, this was the girl, then. "Hi, Jade," I murmured. She smiled at me briefly, her left cheek flashing a huge dimple. But when the dog caught her attention, she ignored me and stared at Marley as though entranced.

"Come on in a minute," Miriam said to me as she headed to the house. Inside, she took Julian off to another room and called, "Just put her on the floor." I gently did as I was instructed, and Jade took off like a shot, crawling faster than I thought a baby should to some toys that formed a huge pile in the living room. *Well, that was easy.*

While Miriam changed Julian's diaper and Marley sat at ease next to me, I perused the huge bookcase in the living room. It held everything from childhood classics to contemporary fiction and more. A collection of Bibles had its own shelf, I noted with appreciation. At home, my lonely copy of the English Standard Version that I had owned as long as I can remember was sandwiched between my copies of Nancy Drew classics and old spiral church cookbooks.

Miriam had grown up in the African Methodist Episcopal Church, AME for short. She had been the administrative assistant of a local congregation, and that's how we first connected. But she had left the position when she had the twins. We church secretaries typically had a lot to chat about.

Miriam was back in no time with a fresh Julian who started pointing and making baby noises to be let loose to play with his sister. I turned from admiring her collection of hymnals.

"So, when's the big move?" I asked, trying to sound upbeat. I wasn't sure that my smile matched my voice.

Miriam stepped closer and put an arm around my shoulders. "We won't be far, my friend. You'll just have to drive that old beast instead of taking the bus." I thanked her with teary eyes and hugged her in return.

"I'd ask you to sit, but I need to start dinner before the rest of the crew gets home." She walked me and Marley to the door. "I can't remember the fella's name, but he looks to be around your age. Easy on the eyes, too, if I must say so myself." With a wink, she added, "Hope you'll be good neighbors!"

Chapter 13

In the morning, Marley and I headed off to the dojo where I could fit in a workout. I packed a blanket in my bag, like Sharon had done for her dog Daisy, and hoped for the best. Marley accompanied me to an empty workout room and snoozed on her blanket while I progressed through my exercises.

Walking home, my new companion had to explore the route, which made the trip significantly longer than the walks I once made alone. But that was okay. Seems I had a new normal. After some housecleaning chores, I packed my sandwich and we made it to the Agathas meeting a little before noon.

When Marley and I walked in, the ladies greeted me and then welcomed Marley as the newest "Agatha." I noticed an extra place had been set for Jane as I took my seat. Marley chose to rest behind me on the floor.

Helen caught my eye. "Your friend will be coming, won't she, Abbey? I'm really eager to hear about her problem."

"Yes, she just has to walk over here from the bakery."

"The bakery?!" Ruthie's eyes lit up. "The one around the corner?"

"There's only one in the neighborhood, Ruthie," said Lillian.

"They have the best scones," Nina added. "Do you think she'll bring some for us to try?"

That stumped me. "I don't know. It would be a nice surprise."

"It would sure beat the peanut butter cookies I brought," Ruthie said.

Jane appeared at the door at that moment, holding a large white box.

"She did!" Marjorie exclaimed. Jane stopped in mid-stride, probably wondering if she'd walked into the right meeting. "Come in, come in, Jane. We were just hoping that you'd bring some goodies." She took the box as Jane sat next to me, and I noticed her peeking inside before placing it on the counter in the kitchenette.

Jane's sandwich, which she unwrapped and placed on her plate, made my mouth water when I saw it. Chicken salad croissant. I looked down at my peanut butter and jelly and sighed. I needed to up my game in the sandwich department.

Following grace, we all caught up on our lives over the past week. The biggest topic, of course, was my adoption of Marley. That led easily into Jane's reason for joining us.

"Should we enjoy our scones while I tell you why I'm here today?" asked Jane.

Nina's eyes lit up. "I'll get them!"

While the dessert was passed around, Marjorie refilled coffee cups. "Start at the beginning, Jane, and just tell us all you know."

"Well," Jane began. "My aunt lives over by the university, and she noticed a few months ago that new people moved in a couple houses away. They appear to have some of those pit bull type dogs. But they aren't walked very much, and the tenants built a huge privacy fence in the backyard." The Agathas quietly absorbed Jane's narrative.

"Aunt Marilyn sits on her front porch a lot, and she's noticed that almost every weekend both the front yard and the street are full of parked cars, and a lot of men stop by, some with their own dogs." Jane sighed. "She doesn't know if she should contact the authorities or not."

"Has she heard any noises suggesting fights in progress?" Ruthie asked.

"No, nothing like that. But she has heard large dogs barking and growling from the fenced-in yard."

Nina sat forward, adjusting her eyeglasses. "I looked up dogfighting online and read that usually the bouts are held in indoor areas like basements."

"That's true," Helen said. "The dogs in the yard are probably chained up."

The ladies remained quiet for a moment until Lillian said, "Those poor dogs, suffering horrendous injuries. And some even die from the attacks. Your aunt definitely needs to call the city or at least the local ASPCA." Everyone at the table agreed.

"And you or your aunt could contact the landlord who owns the house if you think it's still a rental," said Helen. "You can find out that information on the city's property website."

"I would think the police would be right on that," Marjorie added,

"Hunh!" Ruthie said. "The local cops really focus on breaking up dogfighting rings. They come down hard on *those* criminals. But if your car is broken into, forget it. You're lucky to get a cop to file a report. And don't get me started on the parking situation–"

"Okay!" Lillian interrupted. "We're all glad you came today, Jane. Please let us know the outcome, won't you?" She offered a broad smile.

Jane placed her hand to her throat in gratitude. "Thank you so much, ladies. I'll pass on your views to my aunt. I know she'll do the right thing." She looked at the clock on the wall and added, "I need to get back now. My lunch hour is up in five minutes. Thanks again!"

"And thank you for the scones!" Ruthie said.

I walked Jane to the door. "Hopefully, your aunt reporting them will stop it, and they'll move out. Keep me posted."

Jane gave a brief nod. "Will do."

I turned back to the table, surprised to see Marley there, surrounded by the Agathas. Good to know she made friends easily. I watched as Ruthie slipped Marley a small potato chip.

"So, what other mysteries are hovering around us?" I asked. "Anything for us to investigate?" I wanted to know if there were any new problems for us to consider before we left. As a new member, I was still interested in the kinds of troubles the women typically looked into. Marjorie met Helen's eye and I noticed Helen give a slight nod.

"Actually, yes," said Marjorie.

"You know that the church has decided to continue the free Saturday lunch program? Well, it seems there has been quite a lot of food going missing during the week."

Ruthie piped up. "It's the bread."

"Really?" I asked, focusing on Marjorie. I was at first confused, thinking they were referring to the bread used for the Lord's Supper. Momentarily, I felt an uncomfortable silence and realized that five women were looking right at me.

"What? Communion bread? Not me!" I exclaimed. I sat up straight and, hearing my raised voice, Marley did, too.

Lillian chuckled. "No, no, Abbey, not you. If everyone is thinking what I am, we think you'd be the best *detective*, so to speak."

"Since you're here when the rest of us aren't, you know, could you *investigate?*" Ruthie said.

"Oh," I relaxed in relief. "I see. What's been happening?"

Marjorie began by stating, "We're being robbed, that's all!"

Chapter 14

"It's the bread," Nina repeated Ruthie's statement. "Whole loaves!"

"It's odd that nothing else is taken. No peanut butter or jelly, no meat from the fridge," said Helen.

"Wait, some Oreos went missing last week," added Ruthie. She looked around the table and grinned. "That's what I'd take."

"At first we thought it might be a member of the addiction group that meets here on Friday nights," Marjorie continued. "But Lillian stopped over one afternoon and spoke with the member who sets up the coffee and snacks for the group. He said he'd keep an eye out."

"So, would you be able to look around while you're here and see if anything seems unusual?" asked Nina.

"Sure, I'd be happy to," I agreed. The weekend lunch program had proven to be a huge benefit in nourishing local kids, and I'd do anything to find out why it had been targeted. "How long has this been going on?"

"A month now," Nina said. "Marjorie's been running to the store to buy bread every Saturday morning before the kids arrive. It's being donated by church members, so we don't feel as if we can go and ask them to give us more."

"The Women's Society provides the rest of the food," Helen said.

"Okay, I'll look into it."

"Thanks so much, Abbey," Marjorie said. "Oh, and before I forget, we won't be meeting next week because we'll be joining the other members of the Women's Society on a trip to the Sonnenberg Gardens in Canandaigua. You're welcome, to come along, Abbey."

I patted Marley's head and declined, saying, "I think I have another commitment, but thanks."

Before driving home, I decided to check out the fellowship hall where the food program operated. Marley and I took the back stairs to the basement with the daffodil-colored walls. I flipped a light switch and saw about ten banquet tables arranged in a "U" shape, each with eight chairs. I walked past them, and in the kitchen the sandwich ingredients had been set out in an orderly fashion on one long counter.

Four wrapped loaves of white bread and another four of whole wheat, jars of peanut butter and jelly, three packages of chocolate chip cookies, knives, plates and more appeared all ready for Saturday. Deciding to check again tomorrow after work, I turned off the lights and we took off for home.

I was immersed in the latest book by one of my favorite authors when my brother called around nine o'clock.

"Hey! How are you?" I said.

"Okay," Vince answered. "But I want to know how *you're* doing with your gorgeous new housemate. How goes it?"

"Marley and I make quite the pair. She's over on her downstairs bed listening to our conversation." I made kissy lips at her and she closed her eyes. I frowned.

"Downstairs bed? Really?" Vince asked.

"I had to get another because well, you know, one for upstairs and—"

"One for downstairs," Vince finished my sentence. "I get it. How are you two getting along? I mean, as I first-time dog owner, you must have questions, uncertainties…?"

I looked at my phone. *Really?* "Is that condescension I hear? I'm not twelve, for Pete's sake." Then I paused. "Actually…"

"I knew it! Ask me. I've got the answers."

So full of himself. With a huge sigh, I said, "I need to know if I have to get her a crate. She's okay here so far, but if I have to leave her alone, I'm not sure what she might do. She did pee once in the kitchen. But I think that was because I forgot to let her out before I left the house. If I kept her in there, I'd need to block off two doorways."

"You could get a couple of baby gates." Vince suggested. "But, it's really important to see how she reacts to being in a large crate in case you need to leave her with someone or in a boarding situation. Her confinement at the shelter is not really a good gauge."

"Okay, I'll look into that." We spent the next few minutes discussing food, toys, training, and other dog stuff. Eventually I had to beg off. "Work tomorrow. Gotta call it a night."

"I hear ya," Vince said. "Talk soon."

After a brief trip outside, Marley joined me upstairs and curled up on her "upstairs bed."

I smiled. *Nothing wrong with two beds, nothing at all.*

On Friday afternoon I purchased a metal crate for Marley. It took all weekend to train her to feel comfortable enough in it to lie down; we exhausted a full bag of mini treats on that exercise. I kept it set up in a corner of my kitchen so that she would become used to having it around and, hopefully, see it as a place of refuge if needed.

When I stopped in the bakery on the following Monday, Jane looked especially perky, her eyes bright. She said, "Abbey! Did you see the news?"

"No, what?"

"The police broke up the dogfighting ring!" She paused to take my order of a croissant, a blueberry muffin and a dog cookie, filling a white bag.

"Aunt Marilyn found the house's owner online and contacted him. The landlord stopped in at the neighborhood service center and reported her suspicions to the police. Turns out that there were a couple other neighbors who had witnessed the same goings-on."

"Wow, that's amazing. And fast," I said and took my bag and shoved a dollar bill in the tip jar.

"Pretty big doin's for a quiet street, let me tell you. Sirens, flashing lights, the works. And it's all thanks to you and the Agathas! The police said they had already begun investigating, but Aunt Marilyn's call pushed things along." Jane leaned forward on the counter. "Please thank them for us, will you?"

"You got it. We aim to please!"

"Oh! You need to read the article in this week's News. I think you'll recognize a name or two!"

I couldn't wait to tell the ladies. I grabbed a copy of the latest free area newspaper on my way out.

Chapter 15

Two days later on Wednesday afternoon I locked the church office, and Marley and I checked out the fellowship hall to see if anything was amiss with the kids' food. I stopped short in the kitchen when I saw what had been the well-prepared food table. Half the loaves of bread were missing! I counted again. Only four loaves remained, two white, two wheat, out of the original eight.

I pondered this. So, the theft happened between the end of last week's Agathas meeting and now. I hadn't heard any unusual noises during the day, and neither had Marley whose hearing was far more acute. I decided to do some investigating. The ladies did call me a detective, after all.

I first checked all the doors and windows to be sure they were locked. This took some time, but the mission revealed nothing had been mistakenly left unlocked or open. To me, that meant an inside job. *Oh, Abbey, so technical. I must be watching too much crime drama.*

Next, I began checking places in the building where someone could hide. Closets, upstairs classrooms, and even the pastor's study. I started on the top floor and inspected all the rooms. Marley followed me, sometimes taking off on her own to sniff out curiosities. In the second grade Sunday school room, I found her chomping on some leftover animal crackers that hadn't been devoured by the kids. I figured they wouldn't hurt her any, but she did do a number on the cardboard container while opening it. I threw the soggy box in a waste basket.

We explored and had no luck. That left the basement level where I hit the treasure-trove.

As I opened the janitor's closet by the back door, I switched on the overhead light. Two loaves of unopened bread lay prominently on the top back shelf. The missing loaves of wheat bread. I gingerly made my way past the brooms, mop and bucket, vacuum, trash bags and cleansers to reach them.

Pulling them down, I recognized the plastic wrappers as the same brand the food program used. I put them back where I had found them and carefully backed out of the closet so as not to cause anything to come crashing down on my head. Marley followed me to the narthex where I took a seat in one of the usher chairs.

"What should I do next?" I asked Marley. The collie watched me with her pale blue eyes urging me to decide, ready for my next move. Since the bread had already been stolen, I decided to call Marjorie and let her know that she'd have to purchase some more bread before the Saturday lunch crowd arrived. But did I need to tell her where I found the pilfered loaves?

"Yes," I said aloud, convincingly, and rose from the upholstered chair. I had agreed to investigate, which I did. I'd report my findings to Marjorie and let her deal with the results. Not a member of the church, I had no business getting involved with the likely thefts by the church custodian.

At that moment, I heard the sound of keys at the back door. Thinking it would be either the pastor or Mr. Becker, I called out. "Hello!"

I could hear labored footsteps on the stairs, step-step-pause, step-step-pause. Mr. Becker's face appeared, and his thin, arthritic figure made its way into my field of vision.

"Good afternoon, Mr. Becker," I said. "How are you today?"

The elderly custodian did not reply while he caught his breath. After what seemed like a long minute he said, "What are you doing still here? You should get on home." He nodded at the front door behind me.

It was not a friendly suggestion. It was a demand. I half expected him to add, "If you know what's good for you." I never was one who enjoyed being told what I *should* do unless I asked for advice. At that point Mr. Becker took a step toward me which Marley saw as menacing. She growled. Surprised, I looked down. "Marley!" She took a step toward the custodian. We weren't about to be intimidated. Surprised, Mr. Becker's eyes widened slightly, but he didn't back away.

I could hear Mr. Becker breathing loudly through his nose, though he was several feet away from us. His right hand still held his church keys, and they jangled together as though under their own power. He stood his ground. He pointed behind me with his left hand. "Out you go!"

I didn't want to engage any further with Mr. Becker; he was an old man, after all, and I did take his recommendation. But not immediately. Marley and I returned to the church office where after closing the door I placed a call to Marjorie. She was understandably distressed but said she'd discuss the situation with the pastor, and they'd decide how to approach the custodian. I downplayed the interaction between Mr. Becker, Marley and myself. I certainly didn't want to get him into any more trouble than he already was in.

"Oh, thank you so, so much, Abbey," she said. "You don't know how much this means to us, to the church. I'm sure Mr. Becker has a valid need for the bread. Hopefully, we'll be able to give him some assistance." Marjorie and Pastor Cameron would speak with Mr. Becker, and she'd fill me in on the details at Thursday lunch.

"Glad I could help, Marjorie," I said with confidence. "See you in a couple weeks."

The following Tuesday afternoon, I arrived home to see a huge moving van in the driveway of my neighbors Miriam and James. *Oh, no! Not yet!* I hurried over, Marley jogging alongside.

"You're moving already?" I met James at their front door, his arms holding a cardboard box designated "Miranda's Bears." I walked with him to the van.

"Yup." He hoisted the box to a mover who was inside the truck. "If it seems sudden, you're right. The new place is move-in ready, and the movers had a cancellation, so..." He gave me a hug. "We're really going to miss you, Abbey. And I know the kids would have loved playing with your dog. Marley, is it?" He knelt down to pet her.

"Yeah. Let me know when you're settled and we'll come over for a visit. Miriam said you sold to a single man. What can you tell me about him? From an interested neighbor's point of view, you know." I smiled.

James stood. "Let's see. He's real pleasant, intelligent, about your age." He stopped speaking as we heard a crash from inside the house. Both of us turned to look.

"DAD! Mommy dropped the Steuben vase!" Young Dashiell stood in the doorway, horrified, his hand to his mouth, his eyes wild.

James turned back to me, his mouth slack. He ran a hand over his face. "Uh, Abbey—"

"Go, go," I urged. "I'll be in touch." James sprinted inside. With a heavy heart, as much for the move as for the death of the vase, I crossed the street with Marley. "I guess I'll find out about our new neighbor when he moves in," I remarked to Marley. "Let's go get some exercise."

I changed into my sweatpants and we powerwalked to the lake. I had tucked some cash into my pocket to treat ourselves with custard from

Costello's. I included Marley because I discovered whatever flavor I choose is her favorite flavor. It's not really healthy for her, but I figured it isn't for me, either. I only let her have a taste. Her sweet tooth isn't as impressive as mine. We took our time on the pier, basking in the warm, welcome October breeze.

The beach wasn't busy on this autumn weekday afternoon, no teenagers, mainly retired folks and young mothers and fathers again with little children. Marley remained on her leash, though, because after the last time we were here, I didn't trust anyone we might run into.

Strolling the boardwalk with my custard cone, I observed a man using a metal detector on the beach. He seemed quite practiced, swinging the instrument methodically left and right over the sand while walking in a focused, relaxed manner. He glanced up to see me watching.

"Hi, there," I called. "Find anything interesting?"

He removed his large headphones to reveal a head of thick, gray hair tied back in a ponytail. "Not yet. But this isn't really the best time of year to be finding coins and jewelry. That's mainly what I'm after."

I stepped closer, onto the sand. "I suppose summer is best for that, huh?"

"Oh, yeah. You'd be surprised how many people lose their rings and watches. More often I find loose coins, but not huge amounts." He shrugged. "It's mostly just a way to waste time by the water," he grinned. He reached into a jeans pocket and handed me a business card. "Call me if you lose anything metal. I belong to a club and we find lost items for free. Name's Kurt." He replaced his headphones and continued his exploration.

I read his card. "Monroe Metal Detectorists. You Lose, We Find. No Charge." There was a colorful cartoon figure of a man with a metal detector on it, along with Kurt's name and a telephone number. Tucking it into my pocket, I thought, *Hey, you never know.*

I mowed my postage stamp lawn on Wednesday afternoon, hopefully for the final time of the season, and noted several of my neighbors had done the same. We were probably all thinking about the fall mantra: Stabilize the gas in the mower; dig out the snow shovel.

James and Miriam had finished loading the moving van and left for their new home when I returned from the beach, so I hadn't had a chance to say goodbye to the whole family. I didn't feel too bad, though, because I hate goodbyes and I'd be seeing them soon in their new place, anyway, I hoped. Losing contact with good friends was something I tried not to do. For myself, letting go of people who were toxic was just fine. Keeping in touch with the ones who blessed my life was essential. Over the years when friends moved away, we kept in touch through phone calls and letters.

At home I transferred the detectorist's card to my wallet. *What an unusual pastime*, I thought. Sitting in the living room with Marley after dinner, I searched online for metal detectors. There were many available for the beginner, and then pricy ones for the experts. *Wow!* Cheap ones could be bought for $100.00, and the prices climbed to around $1,000.00. I was drawn to the hobby, but not enough to buy a detector.

After that, I looked up metal detecting in general. There were websites about where to go metal detecting, rules to follow, and local clubs to join or contact if you needed help. I saw that Monroe Metal Detectorists was, indeed, listed. That was reassuring, even though I didn't think I'd need them anytime soon.

Yawning, I closed my laptop and noticed the newspaper I'd picked up at the bakery sitting on the table. Thumbing through it, I stopped to read the article about the broken up dogfighting ring. Though not a subject the small arts and entertainment newspaper typically covered, it was notable for the fact that a brother of a city legislator was hugely involved. *Wow!* Now that was news. All the grisly details were there, including some I didn't want to read right before bed. I stared at the accompanying photos and was truly not that surprised to see the face of the man I had encountered on the beach that first day with Marley. He was being walked to a police car, hands cuffed behind his back. Unlike many suspects, he stood tall, facing the camera in defiance. The photo's caption identified him as the brother of the city official. *Well, well, well.*

Marley and I climbed upstairs to call it a night. My favorite thriller author's extraordinary storytelling kept me awake until I gave in and surrendered to the Sandman.

Chapter 16

I dreamed of finding hidden treasures and awoke Thursday morning with my right hand balled into a fist. All I remember is grabbing something sparkly and holding it up for others to admire, *"Ta Da!"* I think I may have said that out loud because Marley was there standing by my bed, looking as quizzical as a dog could.

"Sorry, girlie," I said. "Sometimes I talk in my sleep." I swung my legs over the side of the bed, and she sidestepped them and followed me out of the room. After our routine morning activities, we headed to the animal shelter where we settled in the small office. This weekend was the shelter's Open House. I looked lovingly at Marley who rested serenely on the area rug. Thank goodness all that was behind us.

I was typing up a storm, entering new adoption information, when Mark rapped softly on the doorframe about an hour later. I looked at him and paused. "Hi, Mark! What's up?"

He pulled over a wood desk chair and sat next to me. He sighed, took a hard, obvious swallow and inhaled.

I turned in my chair to face him. "What's wrong? What did I do? I'm so sorry if I—"

"No, no, no," he said, shaking my words away with his hand. "It's about Marley."

My heart turned cold, like it had been immersed in ice water. "Marley? What about her?"

Mark pinched the bridge of his nose and tightly closed his eyes. When he opened them, he said, "A friend of mine was talking with someone last night who told him that his collie has been missing for a couple weeks now."

"No, no…" I murmured.

"The description matches Marley." He took my hand. "Now, the only thing we can do is wait and see if this person notifies us. We aren't in the business of searching for owners of non-microchipped animals."

I took back my hand and reached for my purse. "I, we, have to go. Now. Marley!"

Mark and I both stood, and I snatched Marley's leash.

As I made for the door, I heard him say, "I just wanted you to be prepared in case…"

I drove as fast as the law allowed to the Highland Baptist Church.

Since it was Thursday and the Agathas met at noon, I was expected, but surprised Marjorie and Helen by arriving half an hour before the rest of the group. As Marley and I walked into the parlor, Marjorie looked up.

"Abbey! You're early!" She put down a bowl of pickles. "Are you all right, dear?"

My eyes brimmed with tears. "Marley's owner is looking for her. I don't know what to do." I told Marley to lie down and stay, and then I said to Marjorie and Helen, "I need to think in the sanctuary for a few minutes. Can you watch her?"

"Of course! Certainly!" The ladies shooed me away.

Seated in the front row, I clasped my hands in front of me and looked up, praying for direction. By the time I had completed my plea, my heart rate had slowed and I was no longer overwhelmed by dread. The voice inside calmed me and communicated that it would all turn out okay. *Why is it so hard to believe?*

Collecting my emotions, I remembered to whisper a thank you and returned to the parlor where the rest of the women had gathered. They all watched as I took my place at the table.

"I'm okay now," I said in what I hoped was a soothing manner. I smiled and placed my napkin in my lap.

"Anything we can do?" Lillian asked.

"How about saying grace? I'm mighty hungry." We all laughed and began our meal.

The highlight of the lunch conversation was last week's trip to Canandaigua. The gardens were still lovely, colors hanging on, and the drive had been spectacular. Evidently I'd have to take a trip to the southern tier before the autumn colors faded in the hills. Eventually, the chatter turned to the missing bread. Marjorie took the helm.

"As you know, we asked Abbey to look into the disappearing loaves of bread from the Saturday lunch program." Marjorie took a deep breath. "Abbey informed me Mr. Becker has been taking the loaves."

"What? Really? Why?" The ladies all spoke at once.

Marjorie continued. "I met with Pastor Cameron and she decided to meet with Mr. Becker to see what he needed and if the church could help." She met the other women's eyes. "It turns out he took the bread because his daughter and her four children have moved in with him and his wife. She lost her job and is having trouble finding a new one. And Mr. Becker doesn't make more than minimum wage here."

"Oh," Nina said. "Like Jean Valjean in 'Les Misérables!' He stole bread to feed his starving children."

"But unlike Valjean's situation, the church won't punish him. The children will be fed here at church on Saturdays, and the Women's Society will provide extra food for the family during the week."

"We need to look after our own," Helen said, taking in the women around the table. I realized then that all the women in the Agathas were also members of the church's Women's Society, the guild which focused on benevolence.

"Oh, that's perfect," Ruthie said. "I was wondering what the women were going to do for this year's church contribution."

"Yes, it all works out," added Lillian. "I'm thinking that some of the teens could offer to babysit for Mr. Becker's daughter sometimes. All parents and grandparents need a break once in a while." Agreement was unanimous on that proposal.

I sat back in my chair, appreciating how these women all joined together to make sure people were assisted when their circumstances were not ideal.

"Is there anything else to be addressed today?" Marjorie asked of the group.

Lillian tentatively raised her hand. "I don't know if this is appropriate for the Agathas, but I lost my pearl ring. It was a gift from my grandmother." Her eyes filled. "I just don't know what to do! I can't find it anywhere." She covered her mouth with her hand.

Lillian accepted a tissue Ruthie offered from across the table. "The grandkids and I were at the school playground on Congress Avenue. But it could be anywhere! I've looked at home, turned the car inside out, checked pockets..."

I got up and searched my wallet for the Metal Detectorists business card. I handed it to Lillian.

"Here. When I was at the beach yesterday, I spoke to a man who was using a metal detector to find stuff in the sand. He belongs to this group. His name is on there, Kurt. Call him. His group looks for lost jewelry and coins for people, for free."

"Really? Oh, thank you, Abbey! I'll call him tonight!" Her genuine smile of relief lit up her face.

"Oh, before I forget," I said. "Jane thanks you all for helping with the dogfighting ring. The cops closed it down really fast after the complaints by the neighbors."

"Excellent! Well done! Glad to help!"

Chapter 17

The remaining days of October passed, and I rejoiced in the cooler temperatures and bright autumn colors of the sugar maples and the ginkgoes. Marley and I became a welcomed pair in the neighborhood with our daily walks, and she made many more friends in a few weeks than I had in all the time I had lived there. Halloween was fun this year because the trick or treaters got a thrill being greeted at the door by Marley in a witch's hat.

I got the idea from Jane, who always dressed up for Halloween at the bakery. Her cookies, with their orange, white and black icing were a perennial hit, and I enjoyed every single one that helped lighten my wallet. When I was last there, she updated me on her aunt's experience stamping out the dog fighting ring.

Jane's Aunt Marilyn and her neighbors have welcomed a new family into the home that used to hold dogfighting bouts. Its backyard now contains a huge playset. The kids who live on Marilyn's street seem to have unanimously chosen it as the "popular" house.

"You wouldn't believe the difference on that street, Abbey! It's become such a community. The grass in the front yard around the huge maple tree has even worn away where the kids use it for hide and seek."

The meeting on the first Thursday in November was lively for the Agathas. Seems we all had stories to tell about the number of, or lack of, trick or treaters that came to our doors. At about fifty kids, I thought I had a large amount. The extreme range in different areas surprised me.

Nina and Ruthie, who lived in the suburbs, had the biggest groups with over 100 youngsters each on that Saturday night.

"I almost ran out of little candy bars," Nina said.

"I *did* run out!" Ruthie retorted. "I had to start handing out bags of microwave popcorn!"

Marjorie and Lillian, city residents, had fewer than I had, at around thirty children per household.

Marjorie told us, "There are so many neighborhood parties now, that we seem to get fewer and fewer little ones every year."

Lillian agreed. "And lots of the city kids go to the suburbs. I've heard that they often hand out full-size candy bars! Oh, guess what! I called Kurt and asked him to search for my pearl ring. She flashed her right hand, showing off the gorgeous jewel. He discovered it in the wood chips of the school playground!" After we had finished congratulating her, she added. "I'm so grateful. I've been recommending the Metal Detectorists to all my friends. I even bought a detector to have adventures with my grandchildren."

That Thursday, we didn't have a mystery to solve, but we did have a great dessert made by Lillian out of leftover candy bars.

When I pulled in to my driveway that afternoon, I noticed a tall, lone man walking around the yard of Miriam and Kurt's former home. He was photographing the landscaping with his phone. *Ah, my new neighbor!* Deciding there was no time like the present, Marley and I crossed the road to speak with him. When we reached the sidewalk in front of his house, he looked over at us. Her leash ripped from my hand, Marley charged across the yard to the man.

"Marley!" I chased after my dog.

"Harley!" the man exclaimed. The new homeowner and I looked at each other.

"Abbey?"

"Tom?"

I was transfixed, staring into the deep brown eyes of my fifth-grade crush, Thomas J. Lowell, III.

Chapter 18

I simply could not believe my eyes. Standing in front of me was the person I thought I'd never see again, the boy who made my heart race through eight school years of unrequited love. Tommy Lowell in the flesh. And why was my dog jumping all over him? I resisted the urge to push her away and leap on Tom myself.

As if reading my mind, Tom stopped hugging Marley and stood with arms outstretched. "Abbey Quill! It *is* you! You look fantastic!"

So do you, I thought. I stepped into his arms for a brief embrace, since that was all I could handle in the moment. But I didn't want to let go. My heart pounded so hard I thought he could surely hear it. I was on fire. I stepped back. "'It *is* you.' What do you mean by that?"

"James and Miriam told me a woman named Abbey Quill lived across the street, but I'm not a huge believer in serendipity. Maybe I should rethink my philosophy."

"How do you know Marley's name?" My breathing began to return to normal.

"Marley? I named her Harley." He smiled. "Huh. How come she's with you?"

"I adopted her from the animal shelter a couple weeks ago. She was found tied to a sign post in the city. So, she's *yours?*" I cast a dubious eye to the tail-wagging collie.

"Yeah, believe it or not. I live in Hilton, and a guy was dog sitting while I was out of town. He wasn't careful about leaving the fence gate closed and she escaped." He knelt to rub Marley's neck with two hands.

"I've been searching for her ever since." The collie gazed at him, mesmerized, and he kissed the top of her head.

"You should have had her microchipped." I heard the accusation in my voice, wishing I didn't feel so judgmental. I mean, here was the love of my life with my, *our*, dog. *Our dog?*

Tom had the grace to look rueful. He cleared his throat before saying, "I thought I'd never see her again."

And I thought I'd never see you again. I suppressed that thought and said, "So you're my new neighbor?"

"Sure am." He looked back at the house. "It's a perfect place for me. I love being near the water, and I wanted to be closer to downtown where I work."

"Come on over for a coffee? Or something stronger?" I gestured in the direction of my house. He smiled that smile which had thrilled me when he asked to borrow a pencil in fifth grade. My heart fluttered. Still the same feeling after so many years.

We crossed the street, Tom stroking and talking to *his* Harley, while I held an inner dialogue, trying to come to grips with the idea that I might have to give her up. My mind was racing, and I barely knew what to say next. I edited every thought that popped into my mind. A heaviness invaded my heart. *She's still mine.*

Inside, he assessed my kitchen and settled in a chair. "Nice place you have here."

"Thanks." I held up a bottle of my latest favorite, a pinot gris out of Oregon, and he gave me a thumbs up. I poured us each a glass and joined him. Marley chose a space on the floor between us, nose on her feet, eyes on us as we spoke.

"To old friends," Tom said. We touched glasses.

"So, what do you do for a living?" I asked.

"I develop video games. Unless you play, you probably wouldn't recognize the names."

"Try me," I said.

"Well, the most popular is "Galaxy Steward.""

"That sounds familiar…"

He laughed. "Don't even! You're not a gamer, are ya?"

"No, but my next door neighbors play," I said in my defense. " I'm sure I've heard them talk about it."

He raised his glass to his lips. "You'll have to introduce us."

"Of course." *Joyce and Natalie will never believe this is in a million years.*

"And you? What takes up your time?"

"I'm a church secretary," I murmured. I took a large mouthful of wine.

Tom leaned forward. "A what?"

I smiled and lifted my chin as I said, "A church secretary."

He sat back. "Huh. The class salutatorian is a church secretary." He took a moment to consider the fact. "Full time?"

"No, part time." I noticed his puzzled look. "It's all I need, really. And I like the job. No stress."

"Don't tell me. Independently wealthy?" He smiled, and his white teeth, tanned face, and hair still as black as a raven's wing revealed why I had fallen for this California transplant so many years ago.

When I didn't answer, his face lost its teasing, light-hearted grin. He tilted his head slowly, not believing it. "Really?"

"I won some money in the lottery a few years ago." I sipped my wine and met his eyes. "It happens. You must do pretty well as a video game developer."

"Yes, I do," he admitted. "Hmm. I wouldn't have taken you for a gambler. I'll have to take you with me to Del Lago." We laughed, and I knew why I had never forgotten him and our friendship.

I wanted to address the elephant in the room. "So. What are we going ᵗ do about Harley/Marley? No wonder she responded so quickly to the ᵃme I chose. They sound alike."

"They sure do. I named her after Harley, a character with whom I am *very* familiar because of my work."

"Ah," I smiled. "Marley. Reggae."

"Reggae and religion, huh?" He leaned forward again. "We've got a lot of catching up to do, Abbey Quill." Tom reached across the table and took my hands in his.

We talked of many things that night and didn't come to a decision about Harley/Marley for several days. She stayed with me until Tom moved in across the street two weeks later. Then she had two homes. For a while.

Alibi for Murder

Abbey Quill had been a faithful customer of the "A Through Y" mystery bookstore for a long time, even before she had moved into the Summerhaven neighborhood on the lake. The revealing second part of the name, "Mysteries and More," guaranteed her regular visits to stock up on cute gifts and new reading material. She pushed her pile of books up on the quaint old shop's original oak checkout counter and waited for the clerk to show up.

She was admiring the assortment of handmade stationery displayed in the glass case in front of her when she heard her name.

"Hi, there, Abbey!"

"Omigosh!" Abbey snapped to attention and squinted at the employee standing in front of her. "Ms. Emerson? Is that you?"

"It certainly is, dear." She sniffed. "I haven't changed that much, have I?"

"Oh, no, of course not." Feeling a tad chastised, Abbey said, "Is this where you've been spending time since retiring from the library?"

Julia Emerson reached for the stack of books. "I started here part time, just a few hours a week to keep myself busy. Don't want to stagnate, you know." She placed the first book under the scanner and set it aside. "I really didn't want to volunteer at the library. Been there, done that, as they say."

Abbey unzipped her crossbody purse to remove her credit card as Julia continued scanning the books. She tapped the blue card on the reader, watched it be approved, and replaced it in her wallet.. "How many years were you with the system?"

Tucking the receipt between the pages of the last book, Julia replied, "Forty-five years, can you believe it? Can't say I enjoyed them all. Do you need a bag?" Abbey shook her head and held up her well-used cloth tote from the Tattered Book, a store in Colorado. The bag itself was almost in tatters after fifteen years.

Julia handed Abbey her purchases one by one. "My favorite years, though, were when I was the children's librarian downtown." She sighed and looked into the distance. "Oh, that secret room was something else. It enchanted all the children who crossed its threshold." She scoffed. "But having to deal with the adults. Oh, my, that became unbearable. I'm surprised I lasted as long as I did."

"I remember the secret room well, Ms. Emerson. The woman who helped fill it with dolls from other countries is a friend of mine. A former teacher. Caroline Carlson."

"Yes! I know her, too. We still keep in touch at Christmas." She crossed her arms and leaned forward. She shifted her eyes side to side and said in a conspiratorial whisper, "Just between you and me, Abbey, I bought the bookstore a few months after I left the library. I haven't told anyone outside the family yet. You're the first."

Abbey raised her eyebrows in surprise. "Well, go, you! What a great second chapter this will be!"

"And please call me Julia, Abbey. Now that I'm retired, 'Ms. Emerson' makes me feel old."

"Julia, it is," she smiled. "See you next time, I hope!" With a heavy bag of books, and a wallet that felt none the lighter for spending the money on them, Abbey walked through the parking lot to her car, pulling her coat's collar more tightly around her throat. The late afternoon sky had become slate gray, and the wind gusty, as if predicting a dismal Saturday night ahead. She drove to her little bungalow on the lakeshore that she shared with her boyfriend Tom and made it home just as the downpour let loose.

Abbey opened the door from the garage into the kitchen and inhaled. The aroma of Italian sauce filled the air. Their blue merle collie was excited to see her and greeted her with an enthusiastically wagging tail as Abbey dropped the tote and her purse on the table.

"Heya, Harley Marley!" Abbey gave her some love as Tom tended to the stove. "What smells delicioso?"

"Eh, just plain old lasagna, garlic bread and green salad." He turned, and she saw that he had donned one of her mother's old aprons, the one that said, "Kiss Me, I'm Organic."

Abbey walked over and encircled Tom in a hug. "Mmm, good apron choice," she murmured, and planted a kiss firmly on his lips. Just then, the oven timer's lively tune went off and Tom reached for the pot holders.

"Five minutes!"

Abbey went to wash her hands upstairs, out of Tom's way while he put the finishing touches on dinner. She brushed her long brown hair and braided it quickly before going back downstairs.

Tom was pulling the apron off over his head when she entered the room, and he gestured toward the table where Abbey took a seat. She noticed that Harley had assumed her own customary spot in a corner. The collie never missed a meal, hers or theirs.

As they ate, they discussed their day. Tom, a video game developer, had worked from home. Abbey had spent the day at the Highland Baptist Church, volunteering at the Saturday lunch program for neighborhood kids.

During a break in their conversation, Tom looked in the tote from the bookstore. "A good assortment here. Warner, Comer, Taylor and... Hamilton?"

"She's my cozy fix. Her main character is a basket weaver. I have enough crossword puzzles for now. And I'm almost finished with the one in the *Times*."

"Yeah, I noticed that," he said. "Tell me about that mystery bookstore. What's with the odd name, 'A Through Y'?"

"Oh, now that's really interesting. There was a mystery writer who passed away a few years ago. She wrote detective novels known as the alphabet series. The first one is 'A is for Alibi,' the second is 'B is for Burglar,' and so on, all the way to 'Y is for Yesterday.' Abbey took a sip of her pinot noir. "Well, she died before she could write the last one. I read that she had already chosen 'Z is for Zero' as the title. Her estate won't let a ghostwriter write in her name, so the series ends with Y. Evidently the author didn't want that, or any movies or tv shows to be made based on the series, either."

"Huh. So that's that. No Z."

"No Z."

Tom finished his garlic bread, using it to wipe up some sauce from his plate. "That's a pretty cool name for a mystery bookstore, then."

"I agree. Oh, and get this. Remember little Ms. Emerson, the librarian who just retired? She's working at the bookstore now. Says she doesn't want to stagnate."

He shook his head. "As if anything could cause that woman to slow down. God, she was nosy."

"I know! So irritating," Abbey laughed. "I'm sure the patrons had some choice words to describe her over the years. Heaven forbid you check out a book on the Banned Book list. But listen, she bought the store! Said she hasn't told many people about it."

"Mum's the word." He picked at the remaining casserole and chose a small piece of sausage. He held it at the edge of the table where Harley could see it. She slowly approached and sat next to him. Harley's eyes darted back and forth between the meat and Tom's face. When he quietly said, "Okay," she gently took the morsel in her mouth and returned to the corner to savor it.

Abbey touched Tom's hand that was resting on the table. "Have I thanked you for training her so well? She's such a lady. And smart, too."

He laced his fingers through hers. "Collies are intelligent dogs, and she was the pick of the litter. But I'll accept the credit." He smiled into Abbey's eyes. "My mother always told me to make smart choices." Abbey's eyes smiled back.

On the following Monday, Abbey stopped at the Brooks Bakery for her usual pastry and coffee before opening the church office. Jane, the proprietor, began pouring Abbey's coffee before the secretary had reached the counter.

"Morning, Abbey, what can I get for you? We have croissants fresh out of the oven."

She examined the goodies behind the glass. "One of those, for sure, and um, a cherry Danish. And a couple black and whites for home, please."

Jane filled the white bag. "Do you want the cookies separate?"

She sighed. "Yes, you'd better. Too tempting."

"I got ya."

Abbey was stuffing a dollar into the already full tip jar when Jan said, "Did you see the news this morning? There was a homicide in the 'A Through Y' bookstore Saturday night!"

Her hand stilled. "What? Who? What happened?"

"An employee, Julia Emerson. She was found on the floor near the café inside on Sunday morning by the manager when he opened up. Hit her with the standard 'blunt instrument.'" She used air quotes round the two words.

Abbey felt the tears welling up at the bad news. "I was just there on Saturday," she said. "I've known Ms. Emerson for years. She started working in the store after her retirement from the library." She clutched her bags of pastry. "I, I can't believe this." She turned to go.

"Don't forget your coffee." Jane nudged it toward the counter's edge. "And I'm sorry for breaking it to you like this. It's so hard losing an acquaintance, especially to murder."

Abbey checked the news several times each day before the Agathas meeting on Thursday. The Agathas were a group of six women who met once a week to discuss and solve any problem or quandary that arose in their day-to-day lives. On Wednesday it was reported in the news that Ms. Emerson's brother, Robert Emerson, was being held for the crime. The type of murder weapon had not been identified, and Mr. Emerson was maintaining his innocence. The death of the well-known librarian who had had so much life left to enjoy was the main topic at the Agathas' lunch that week.

All the women of the Agatha group were in attendance. Marjorie, Helen, Lillian, Nina, Ruthie and Abbey were all eager to discuss the murder. The conversation around the attack was lively.

During the dessert of cherry crunch, Nina said, "If Mr. Emerson says he was at a gathering Saturday evening, then someone must have seen him. Where was he, again?"

"He says he and his daughter Ivy were at some talk about the Erie Canal that night. Abbey said. "It was held at the Historical Depot."

"That canal museum? It's not open in November, is it?" asked Helen.

"Usually, no, but it was available specially for that," Lillian spoke up. "I was at the presentation. About forty people were there. What does he look like?"

Ruthie took out her cell phone and looked up a recent article on the murder. "Here he is. His daughter, too." She handed the phone to Lillian.

Lillian studied the two photos. "I do remember them! I sat in the back row so I could leave the room if I needed to without much distraction. And, those two were sitting a couple rows ahead of me on the aisle like I was."

"What do you remember about that night, Lillian?" Abbey asked. "Not about the Erie Canal, but about *them*. Anything stand out?"

Lillian returned Ruthie's phone and sat back. "Well, he didn't move much, if at all, but *she* kept going over to the refreshments table for cookies and drinks. It was kind of annoying, really. I'm surprised no one's come forward about seeing them there."

"Was there any pre-registration required?" Helen asked. "Maybe the authorities could check a list."

Lillian shook her head. "No, not for that talk. We didn't get any handouts or anything, either. There was one thing, though. I recall thinking that with all she was drinking, the girl, Ivy, should have to use the facilities. She drank lots of lemonade! And she finally did. Leave, that is. I was glad she left because I could finally pay attention to the program without her moving back and forth in my line of vision."

Marjorie asked, "Did she come right back, or was she gone a long time? It might be important."

"Now that you mention it, she left a little more than halfway through, and I didn't see her again until we were leaving and she met up with her father in the entrance hall. They were having a heated conversation. I thought I heard him say something like, 'Where have you been?' but I can't be certain. I wanted to get home before the rain started up again."

The Agathas were quiet for a minute. Then Abbey spoke. "So Robert may be innocent, but his daughter doesn't seem to have an alibi."

"But why would she want to kill her aunt?" Ruthie asked. "What's the story here?"

Lillian frowned and looked around the table. "I guess this means I have to call the police, doesn't it? Or Crimestoppers?"

"Crimestoppers," Ruthie said. "I'll look up the number for you." She handed her phone to Lillian after a few quick touches on the screen. "Here."

"Thanks, I'll call now. Before I go home."

The police, of course, were very interested in speaking with Lillian. They wasted no time coming to see the ladies at the church. Later, when it was ascertained that Ivy had no alibi for the evening of her aunt's death, Julia's niece broke down and admitted to killing her.

Local news outlets carried the story in detail. When Julia retired she had used the funds inherited from her parents to purchase "A Through Y." When Ivy learned this, she was enraged. She thought her aunt was well off enough in her own right and was going to give *her* the money. On Saturday, Ivy left the presentation about the Erie Canal early, as Lillian had noticed, and took a hired car to the bookstore. When the two women were alone, Ivy confronted her aunt. She had been counting on her aunt's legacy to help fund her own startup business as a destination wedding planner. However, Julia had never promised any such funding of her niece's business venture. After killing her aunt, Ivy returned to the Depot just as it was letting out.

Thanks to the media, by the time the Agathas met the next week, everyone knew the facts. The members were very much aware that if not for Lillian, a guilty person might have gotten away with murdering a woman who had been a prominent member of the community for many years. But the ladies were curious about one thing.

"So, tell me," Marjorie said. "Does anyone know what Ivy hit Julia with? What was the blunt instrument?"

The women had a few suggestions for the murder weapon. "A bookend?" "A candle?" "A carved bust of an author?"

"Abbey," Nina said, "did you happen to speak to your friend in the police? Officer Polito, isn't it? Surely, he'd tell you something."

"I did, yes, and he told me what happened," Abbey said. "Ivy Emerson killed her aunt by striking her in the head with a ceramic mug. The cup had 'I Have an Alibi' printed on it."